**PRAISE FOR**
*Prince Iggy and the Kingdom of Naysayer*

"A lonely boy learns how to stand up against a cast of mean bullies in Fynn's debut middle-grade novel... There's plenty of knockabout farce to enjoy with Iggy's new friends...The underlying message that bullying never pays is handled with skill, and a humorous approach keeps the story light. The black-and-white illustrations resemble watercolor sketches and possess a rustic charm that complements the tale. An entertaining fantasy with a quirky, inventive storyline that shows how things invariably turn out badly for bullies."
– *Kirkus Reviews*

"An excellent book. Full of suspense, humor, and fantasy. This storybook is one to treasure. The illustrations are cute, the story is creative, and every little thing makes it the perfect children's book. The plot has unexpected turns and twists and will keep readers flipping through pages...The book is going to be devoured by readers of any type, whether they're looking for some fun fiction, a comical read, or a page-turner."
– *San Francisco Book Review*

"Anyone who has  Prince *Iggy and the Kingd* sages

of perseverance and resilience while weaving an entertaining yarn...What saves the story from becoming an all-too-familiar good-versus-evil tale is the cast of eccentric characters that shows up to assist Iggy...Fynn's writing gets more playful with the introduction of each new character...Fynn is adept at making scenes come to life...readers will pick up some important lessons in self-esteem...Ultimately, readers will feel good about Iggy's triumph over his bullies and look forward to future adventures from this unlikely adolescent hero."
– *Foreword Clarion Reviews*

"A bewitching rag to riches story... incorporates magic, suspense and surprises...the story's messages about confidence and the power of friends and friendships are clear...*Prince Iggy and the Kingdome of Naysayer* is a charming story about finding out who you are and following your heart." – *IndieReader Approved*

# PRINCE IGGY
## & THE KINGDOM OF NAYSAYER

By Aldo Fynn

Illustrated by Richie Vicencio

To Pierce
the Zombie Boy
Hope you enjoy

Richie

## Also by Aldo Fynn:

*Prince Iggy and the Tower of Decisions*

*Legend of the Great Pooping Bird*

*Waldo Battles the Fly*

# PRINCE IGGY
## & THE KINGDOM OF NAYSAYER

By Aldo Fynn

Illustrated by Richie Vicencio

*For Tabitha*

# Chapter 1

In the kingdom of Naysayer there was a large, gloomy building. The building was painted black, like the darkest night, and had many towers that spiraled high into the air. Ugly, thick iron bars covered every one of its many windows, and an imposing ironstone wall circled its vast courtyard. This building had such a miserable air, and was so dreary in its appearance, that even the sun refused to shine down on it. Instead, every day of the year, a dark thundercloud hovered over the building's tallest tower, turning everything down below or inside the color gray.

This horrible building was called the Naysayer Academy. This was where all the boys and girls of the kingdom of Naysayer were forced to live and study. Once admitted to the academy, the children of Naysayer could never leave. They spent every single day walking the academy's long, dreary halls to class.

It was a very sad way for a child to grow up... but it was the saddest of all for a young boy named Iggy.

# Chapter 2

Iggy looked down at the cold, lumpy porridge Ms. Heavybody plopped into his bowl, and began to feel sick.

"Take your porridge and move on!" shouted the cafeteria lady.

In the Naysayer Academy, children were fed porridge for breakfast, lunch, and dinner—every day of the year. Although the porridge was always cold and very lumpy—and on some days even a strange brownish-green color—most students were usually too hungry to complain.

"What's wrong with you?! Take your porridge and move on already!" shouted the wart-covered Ms. Heavybody, annoyed that Iggy was holding up the line.

"It's—it's just that yesterday's porridge made me really sick," Iggy finally said. "Is there any chance I could just get some toast? The toast can be all burned up, moldy, and stale. I don't care. I just think if I have any more porridge I might…I'm afraid I might die."

Suddenly Ms. Heavybody reached over her

counter and picked Iggy up by one arm. "I'll let you know something, you little good-for-nothing," she snarled, showing her many rotten teeth. "My porridge hasn't killed anybody since October of last year. Now either you eat my porridge or you don't eat anything at all!"

Iggy looked away. Ms. Heavybody's porridge may not have killed anybody since October, but he wasn't so sure about her breath.

"Stop being so annoying, Iggy! We're hungry!" shouted one of his classmates.

Iggy turned his head. A long line of hungry kids stared at him as they waited their turn to eat.

Iggy sighed and said, "Fine, I'll eat the porridge."

"That's what I thought," said Ms. Heavybody as she dropped him back on the ground. "Next in line!"

Iggy picked up his tray and stepped away from the counter. He walked toward a long table where all the Naysayer children sat and ate. He watched as his fellow students greedily scooped up mouthfuls of porridge from their tiny bowls.

As usual, Iggy scanned the long, crowded table for a place to sit.

"Keep walking, stink head."

Iggy turned around and saw Teddy. Teddy was the largest kid in school and definitely the meanest. "We don't need you stinking up our table," he said, disgusted.

"I don't stink," said Iggy. "I washed myself three times last night to make sure."

"Well, you should have made it four. Now keep walking! You know this isn't your table." Teddy then bumped his tray against Iggy's.

Not wanting to get into another fight, Iggy turned and walked toward a small, empty table in a far-off corner of the cafeteria. He sighed deeply as he put down his tray and took a seat. Iggy did not know why, but nobody at the Naysayer Academy liked him. At first, he thought it was because he wasn't as smart as everybody else, but then he realized the other kids also made fun of the way he looked.

"Watch out! Here comes vomit face!" some of the kids would shout as he walked past them in the hallway.

But that wasn't all. The kids also made fun of the way he smelled. And this was something he had tried very hard to change. As Iggy had just informed Teddy, every night, while all the other children in the academy were sleeping, he would step out of bed and tiptoe across the cold marble floor toward the boys' bathroom. There, in the middle of the night, he would scrub his entire body with soap—sometimes even two or three times—until he was positive there was no way he could smell bad. But no matter how many times he washed himself, the next morning, somebody would always tell him he stank.

"Maybe there isn't a reason why the other kids don't like me. Maybe they just don't like me because of who I am. But I can't change who I am," Iggy thought to himself. "Although I really wish I could."

Iggy pondered his loneliness. Then, out of the corner of his eye, he saw something squirm in his bowl of porridge. He took a closer look and saw little black tentacles swirling about. He reached down and gasped as he pulled a big black cockroach out of his porridge. He held the insect up by its twisting feelers and watched as it tried to break free. As he examined the cockroach, he had an interesting thought…He wondered if the cockroach had a mother and father. He then wondered if perhaps the cockroach was like him, and didn't know whom its mother and father were. He _then_ wondered if the cockroach was just like him and was also very lonely. Perhaps the cockroach was so lonely it might even want to be his friend. Iggy held the cockroach up close to his face.

"Okay, Mr. Cockroach. I'm going to put you down on the table and let you free. I would also like to extend my offer of friendship. I think you and I could have a lot in common."

Sadly, the second Iggy placed the cockroach down on the table and let it loose, it quickly darted off the table, plopped onto the floor, and scuttled toward a crack in a nearby wall. "I guess I wouldn't want to be my friend either," Iggy muttered as he watched the cockroach disappear.

"Hey, butt face!" somebody shouted.

Iggy looked up and saw Teddy hovering over him. As usual, he did not look happy.

"I'm going to beat you up after school!"

"Why this time?" asked Iggy, sighing.

"Because you're ugly and stupid and I say so, that's why!"

"That's what you said last week," said Iggy.

"Well, nothing's changed!" Teddy yelled.

Teddy then snatched Iggy's bowl of porridge and took it back to the other table. Iggy sat there, hungry, and watched as Teddy shoved a huge spoonful of porridge into his mouth. Then, as Teddy licked the last helping of porridge from his spoon, Iggy noticed the other children sitting at the table pointing and laughing.

Iggy wished he had left the cockroach in his porridge after all. "Then again," he thought, "Teddy probably eats bugs for breakfast. And that wouldn't be a nice thing to do to the cockroach."

# Chapter 3

Iggy sat by himself in the back of the classroom. Going to class made him nervous because he had a hard time keeping up with the other students. Often he would get so frustrated he would spend most of his time just staring out the window. Today, however, something blocked his view. A black crow had perched itself outside the window near his desk. Iggy felt like the crow was studying him very closely. Then he noticed the crow had a silver chain wrapped around its black feathery neck. From the chain hung a bright red amulet.

"Well, that's rather odd," Iggy thought as he looked at the amulet around the crow's neck. Then Iggy looked down at his hand. On his right hand, he wore a silver ring with a red stone in the center. The stone was the same exact color as the amulet around the black crow's neck.

Iggy's ring had always been a mystery. He had no idea how he got it. Perhaps his mother and father had given it to him, but he couldn't be sure since he had no memory of his parents. All he knew was that none of the other kids had rings. This was probably another reason they didn't like him.

Last year, Teddy had tried to take his ring, but Iggy bit Teddy's ear until he gave it back. That's how much the ring meant to him.

Iggy leaned over his desk and took a closer look at the shiny red amulet around the bird's neck. Suddenly, the bird crowed, flapped its wings, and took to flight. Iggy leaned farther over his desk and watched the crow soar high into the sky, then disappear into the dark, gray cloud that hung over the academy.

Startled, Iggy heard a loud SMACK!

"Iggy, pay attention!" screeched Miss Spitfire.

Iggy turned and saw Miss Spitfire, the tall, thin headmistress of the academy, standing in the front of the classroom. She firmly clutched her wooden walking stick in her wrinkled hand. Next to Miss Spitfire stood a short, pudgy man dressed in a red robe and wearing a golden crown. "This is no way to behave in front of King Naysayer," hissed the headmistress.

Iggy quickly dropped back into his chair. Miss Spitfire grimaced as she pushed her glasses up her crooked nose. She turned to the short king standing beside her. "I'm afraid, Your Highness, _that_ young boy is one of our more challenged students. He's not all there, to put it mildly."

Iggy had forgotten that today King Naysayer, the ruler of the kingdom of Naysayer, was visiting the academy to see how his students were progressing. Iggy noticed the king's round, fleshy face had a thin, peculiar mustache, and the king was staring straight at him.

"If you don't start paying attention, Iggy, I'll add one more lump to the back of your head," snapped Miss Spitfire.

"Yes, Miss Spitfire," said Iggy as he sat straight up in his chair. Iggy felt a cold shiver run through his entire body.

"Now, class, tomorrow, as we all know, is the king's forty-fifth—"

"Uh-hum," coughed King Naysayer.

"I mean, twenty-fifth birthday."

"That's better," said King Naysayer.

"And as a special birthday present, I thought we would show Our Royal Highness all the wonderful things you have learned here at the academy. Let's start with you, Teddy. Can you tell King Naysayer why it's not good to share?"

Teddy's pimply face broke into a smile. "That's easy, Miss Spitfire. It's not good to share because if you share, it means you get less."

"Good job as usual, Teddy."

"Now, how about this one?" continued Miss Spitfire. "Can anyone tell me when you should be honest?"

All the children—that is, all except Iggy—eagerly raised their hands. Iggy always found it difficult to remember the answers to Miss Spitfire's questions. It was like his brain was telling him one thing, but his heart was saying another. He had a hard time deciding between the two.

"How about you, Clarisse?" said Miss Spitfire as her crooked finger pointed to a pretty girl with blonde hair sitting in the first row. "Can you tell King Naysayer when you should be honest?"

Iggy thought Clarisse was the prettiest girl in school. He watched as she nodded yes to Miss Spitfire, looked at King Naysayer, and nervously smiled. "You should only be honest, Your Highness, when you know being honest means you will get something in return. If you won't get anything in return, then being honest isn't worth it. Lying is always the best policy."

Iggy watched the short king waddle to Clarisse's desk. The king raised himself onto the tips of his toes so he was eye level with the pretty young girl.

"Good job, young lady," said King Naysayer. "I see a very bright future in store for you."

Iggy noticed Clarisse blush as she lowered her eyes.

"Now, whom should I ask next?" said Miss Spitfire as she skimmed the sea of raised hands with her crooked index finger. "How about…"

"This boy," interrupted King Naysayer as he wobbled down the center aisle of the classroom, heading in Iggy's direction. Iggy pushed his body farther back against his chair as he watched the king approach.

"What's his name again?" asked the king as his piercing dark eyes honed in on Iggy.

"Iggy, Your Highness, our worst student," said Miss Spitfire as she hurried behind the king, rapidly tapping her walking staff on the floor. Then she whispered into the king's ear, "He's the one who washed up on our shores all those years ago."

"Ah yes," said the king as he eyed Iggy. "I remember you. A baby sent out to sea. You must consider yourself rather lucky to have wound up in Naysayer?"

Miss Spitfire whacked Iggy's desk with her staff. "Answer, boy!"

"Yes, Your Highness," Iggy said.

"I thought so," said the king. "Well, according to Miss Spitfire, you are the worst student in the academy. Is that true?"

Iggy looked down at his desk. He felt his hands get clammy and beads of sweat trickle down the back of his neck.

"I—I—I guess so."

"Well, that's not something you should be proud of, is it?" said the king with a giggle.

"I guess not," Iggy said softly.

Then, the king's eyes began to sparkle.

"Oh my…what's this?" he said rather excitedly.

Iggy felt King Naysayer's cold, pudgy hand

suddenly touch his. The king had noticed Iggy's ring. The ring began to sparkle. Iggy watched as the king's eyes widened.

"I want that!" said the king as he tried to pull the ring off Iggy's finger. Iggy quickly pulled back his hand. The king hadn't expected that.

"Well, well, well…" he said. Then, with a devilish grin, the king turned to Miss Spitfire. "Miss Spitfire, I have a question for this young boy."

"Of course, Your Highness," said Miss Spitfire, nodding. She smacked Iggy's desk and turned to the other students. "Class, let's hope Iggy answers correctly, because if he doesn't, none of you will get any porridge for dinner tonight."

Iggy's classmates murmured in annoyance.

"You better get this right, Iggy, or I am going to beat you ten times over!" shouted Teddy from the front of the classroom.

"Silence!" yelled Miss Spitfire. "Well, it looks like today is your lucky day, Iggy. What's your question, Your Royal Highness?"

"My question is this," said King Naysayer. Suddenly he jumped onto Iggy's desk and pointed to the ring on Iggy's hand. "To whom does this ring belong?"

"You're a real idiot if you can't get this one," muttered Teddy as he turned in his seat with disgust.

"Silence," shouted Miss Spitfire again. "Go ahead, Iggy. Answer King Naysayer's question."

Iggy watched King Naysayer lick his wet lips as his body twitched with anticipation. He eagerly rubbed his hands together as he asked again, "Well, boy, to whom does this ring belong?"

Iggy looked down at the bright red ring on his finger. The palms of his hands were soaking from sweat. He looked out the window. He wished he was like that black crow and could fly up into the big sky. He knew the answer to the question. The ring belonged to him. It was the _only_ thing that belonged to him.

"Time's up!" squealed the king as he bent down and grabbed Iggy's hand. Iggy tried to pull his hand back, but the king would not let go. The king's face was now inches from his own, and he could see his nervous reflection in the king's eyes.

"I'll ask you one last time, boy!" shouted the

king. "To whom does this ring belong?!" The king yanked on the ring, trying to dislodge it from Iggy's finger.

Iggy pulled in the other direction.

"It—it—it belongs to me!" shouted Iggy.

WHACK! A sharp pain suddenly shot through the back of Iggy's head.

Iggy felt the ring slide off his finger.

After hitting him with her walking stick, Miss Spitfire said, "Wrong, as usual…"

Iggy closed his eyes and fought back the tears. When he finally opened them, he looked up and watched King Naysayer cram the bright red ring onto his pudgy finger. The king marveled at it and began giggling with glee. Then he jumped off Iggy's desk.

"It's quite beautiful, I must say. I'll consider this an early birthday present from you to me," said the king as he admired the ring. Then he looked straight at Iggy. "Do you know what the right answer to that question was, young boy?"

"No," said Iggy as he looked back down at his desk, rubbing the back of his head and wishing he could just disappear.

"_Me._ The ring belongs to _me_," said the king. "Everything in this kingdom belongs to me."

King Naysayer pulled on the lapels of his robe, took one more look at his shiny new ring, and then motioned to Miss Spitfire. "Well, I think I've seen enough here, Miss Spitfire. Good job turning this young group of children into well-rounded members of our society. I trust I'll see you at my birthday celebration?"

"Of course, Your Highness," said Miss Spitfire.

"Good, till then."

King Naysayer quickly waddled out of the room. Just as he left, a bell rang, signaling the end of class. The students quickly got up and shuffled past Iggy's desk, each one giving him a cold, deadly stare.

"Remember, children!" shouted Miss Spitfire. "Because of Iggy, you won't get any dinner tonight."

Iggy was rubbing the back of his head, trying to relieve the pain, when he noticed Clarisse—the pretty young girl with blonde hair—standing next to his desk. Two other girls stood behind her. For the past year, Iggy wanted to invite Clarisse to eat lunch with him, but he could never muster the courage. Now, as he looked into Clarisse's bright blue eyes, he noticed a strange feeling in his stomach.

"Tell him," said one of the girls to Clarisse.

Clarisse looked at Iggy. Iggy felt the strange feeling in his stomach now move up to his chest.

"You know what, Iggy?" Clarisse finally said.

"What?" Iggy asked, awkwardly smiling.

"You really stink," Clarisse softly muttered, as she lowered her head and walked away. The two girls standing behind Clarisse stuck their tongues out at Iggy and then followed her.

Iggy sighed. He was the only person left in the room. The pain from his head had started to pass.

He wiped a tear from his eye. He sighed again and looked at his right hand. The one thing in his lonely world that belonged to him had been taken away. After a few moments had passed, Iggy slowly raised his tiny, thin body up from his desk. He then lifted his droopy arm and took a big sniff of his armpit. He couldn't smell anything.

# Chapter 4

Iggy stood perfectly still on the school playground. A circle of children surrounded him. He kept his head down and did not move a muscle. His eyes focused on a black cockroach that poked its head out of the sand a few feet from him. By focusing on the cockroach, he hoped to ignore the nasty things being shouted at him.

"You're the dumbest kid that ever existed!" screamed a boy to his left.

"You're really, really, and I mean *really*, ugly," added a girl to his right.

"I can smell you a mile away," said another kid.

"You're the most useless kid that ever lived!" said another.

"You've got bad skin," added one more.

"You're fat!" cried somebody from the back of the crowd.

"I wouldn't be your friend, even if you paid me!" shouted a boy as he threw up his hands.

"I wish you didn't exist!" cried somebody behind him.

And on…and on…it went.

As each new insult was shouted, Iggy stood perfectly still, simply staring at the cockroach. He was certain it was the same cockroach he had rescued from his porridge at breakfast. The cockroach looked up at Iggy. Its feelers twirled around its head. Iggy wondered if the cockroach was also shouting insults at him. "I guess it's a good thing I don't speak cockroach," thought Iggy. Then all of sudden, the cockroach buried its head into the sand and disappeared.

The insults continued. Iggy tried not to listen to the children. If he did, he would start to cry. Then all the kids would make fun of him for being a crybaby.

"Enough!" Iggy heard somebody shout from outside the circle.

"Thank goodness," Iggy sighed hopefully.

He looked up from the ground. He saw the kids in front of him turn around. His hope quickly faded, however, when he saw Teddy shove several kids out of his way and walk toward him, looking meaner than ever.

"Let's get this over with!" hissed Teddy, clenching his teeth, his eyes bulging like a mad bulldog's.

All the kids around Iggy began to cheer. They loved fights!

"Put 'em up!" shouted Teddy as he began pumping his fists.

Iggy did not move. He did not say a word. He was too tired. At that moment, he wished he were tiny like that cockroach and could disappear into the playground sand.

"Come on, Iggy, put 'em up!" shouted somebody from the crowd.

"I don't want to fight," muttered Iggy.

"You don't have a choice," yelled Teddy as he moved in closer.

"Yes, I do. I don't have to fight," Iggy argued softly.

"You do too!" shouted someone else from the crowd. Then one of the kids shoved Iggy. He fell forward. He slowly got up. But just as he was about to stand up straight, a girl pushed him, and he stumbled back onto the ground.

"You have to fight!" the girl shouted.

"No, I don't!" Iggy shouted back. "I don't have to fight just because you say I have to!"

"According to Miss Spitfire, fighting is good for you. It builds character!" yelled Teddy.

"I think Miss Spitfire is an idiot!" Iggy shouted back at Teddy, his face suddenly red with anger.

Everyone was silent. None of the students had ever heard such a thing. Miss Spitfire couldn't be wrong; she was the headmistress of the Naysayer Academy.

"You're a loser, Iggy," said Teddy finally, still pumping his fists. "That's why your parents didn't want you."

Iggy didn't respond. He slowly got up from the ground. He brushed some sand off his knees.

"I'm getting tired of this," Teddy said.

"Thank goodness," Iggy sighed. He watched as Teddy walked away. Iggy did not want to get beaten up again but then realized he would have no such luck. Teddy quickly turned around and charged at him, his right fist flying toward him like a huge meteorite. Before he could blink, Iggy felt a crushing surge of pain rush through his head.

All the boys and girls watched as Iggy's small body floated into the air and then fell to the ground with a thud.

"Ow!" cried Iggy. Bells rang through his ears. His head felt like it was stuck in a jar. He squeezed his stinging eyes tightly.

Teddy and the rest of the children circled him. They looked down at him with disappointment. They had expected more of a fight, but as usual, Iggy let them down.

"Now what do we do?" a boy asked Teddy.

"We could hang him upside down from the flagpole!" shouted a girl.

"Nah...we've already done that," said someone else.

"We could light his underwear on fire!" recommended a boy.

"We did that last week; don't you remember?" said Teddy, shaking his fist.

"We could shove his head down the toilet," eagerly suggested someone else.

"We did that too," shouted Teddy, now getting annoyed that they were running out of ideas. He pointed to Clarisse, who was standing in the back of the crowd. "What do you think, Clarisse? You're the smartest girl in school. Come up with a new way to torture Iggy!" Teddy commanded.

All the kids turned and stared at Clarisse.

"Yeah, Clarisse," said one of the girls. "If you're so smart, come up with something new."

Iggy, who still lay on the ground, struggled to open his burning red eyes when he heard Clarisse's name mentioned. When he finally looked up, he saw Clarisse bent over and looking down at him. Her face was blurry at first, but her pretty features slowly came into focus. "I'm sorry, Iggy," he heard her whisper.

"Sorry for what?" Iggy wanted to say, but his jaw hurt too much to speak.

He then saw Clarisse stand up straight and shout to the rest of the kids, "Why don't we throw him out with the rest of the garbage?"

The kids grew silent as they looked at Teddy. Iggy couldn't believe what he had just heard.

"Sounds like a plan to me." Teddy shrugged. He ordered the kids to pick Iggy up and carry him toward the trash well at the far end of the school courtyard. The trash well was where garbage from the academy was disposed of.

As Iggy felt himself being lifted and carried toward the well, he tried to break free, but there were just too many hands holding on to him.

"Let me go! Let me go!" he begged, but the other students were too busy singing to hear him:

*"Into the trash well you must go!*
*That is your fate, don't you know!*
*Because you smell like rotten toes,*
*Into the trash well you must go!"*

When they reached the trash well, Teddy lifted the heavy wooden lid, and with one big heave, the children tossed Iggy down the well. Iggy dropped more than twenty feet before he finally landed on a pile of rubbish.

"Sweet dreams!" Teddy shouted from above. The lid slid back over the well, and Iggy was trapped in the dark.

"Get me out of here!" Iggy shouted. He banged his hands against the well's brick wall. "Get me out of here!" But nobody replied. He stopped banging the wall when he faintly heard the children singing as they headed back into the academy:

> *"Into the trash well you must go!*
> *That is your fate, don't you know!*
> *Because you smell like rotten toes,*
> *Into the trash well you must go!"*

Then, after a few moments, there was just silence.

Slowly, the smell of the rotten garbage reached Iggy's nose. "Now, this really stinks," he thought to himself. The stench and his throbbing head made him nauseated and tired.

"I can't take this anymore." He sighed. He closed his eyes. He tried to forget he was stuck at the bottom of a well filled with trash. Although he had never been there, Iggy tried to picture himself on a beach or a mountaintop. But when he opened his eyes, he saw that he was still stuck inside the well, and the smell of the trash had started to make his stomach churn. Iggy began to cry.

All the tears he had held back because he didn't want to be made fun of were finally unleashed. He cried and cried, for what seemed like hours.

"I can't take this anymore," he said to himself again and again.

And then Iggy made a wish with all of his heart. A wish so deep that he thought his body was going to explode because he wanted it so badly.

"I wish I wasn't me," he said softly out loud. "I wish with all my heart I was someone else."

That night, as all the children of the Naysayer Academy fell asleep in their beds, Iggy fell asleep surrounded by garbage.

# Chapter 5

**"I**s there anybody down there?" asked a loud whisper from above.

Iggy slowly opened his eyes. He must have fallen asleep for quite some time. His head still ached from Teddy's punch. As he took a deep breath, he coughed from the nauseating stench of the rubbish.

"Can anybody hear me down there?" asked the voice again.

Iggy looked up and saw the silhouette of a man peering down at him.

"Yes. I'm down here! Could you help me up?!" asked Iggy.

"I'll have you out of there within a snare's hair. Don't you worry."

The man lowered down a rope. Iggy took the rope into his hands and began to climb out of the well.

"Easy does it now, Your Highness," the man whispered.

"Your Highness? Does he know who he's talking to?" Iggy wondered as he climbed the rope.

Once he reached the top of the well, Iggy thanked the man and wiped some of the rotten food and other trash off his clothes. He then looked around the courtyard. It was the middle of the night, and everyone in the academy was sound asleep. The moonlight cast long shadows across the ground, and the eerie silence of the night was interrupted only by the cackle of a crow resting on the man's shoulder.

"To think of Your Highness laying in such filth at the bottom of a well…well, it makes me want to bash some skulls in, it does!" exclaimed the stranger.

Iggy realized this man did not sound like any of the teachers he knew at the academy. And through the shadows, he could tell he didn't look like any of the other teachers either. The man had a very long beard and wore a long black coat. His hair was in complete disarray, like it had been hit by lightning a thousand times. Then Iggy noticed the man had only one leg. Where his right leg should have been was a stump made out of wood. Iggy thought perhaps the man was a new teacher he had not yet met.

"CAWWW!" screeched the crow from atop the man's shoulder.

"Quiet, Napoleon!" the man warned the bird. "Or you'll wake up the whole kingdom."

Iggy looked at the bird. Through the darkness,

he could faintly see a red amulet glimmering around its black feathery neck. This was the same crow he had seen earlier in Miss Spitfire's class!

"Are you a new teacher at the academy?" asked Iggy.

"Am I a new teacher at the academy?" the man repeated in a gruff voice. "Hells no. I'm Captain Bartholomew Swell, Your Highness, and I am here to rescue you. Now, if you don't mind, time is in very short supply. We must ride out of here like a bat out of hell."

"Why do you keep calling me that?" asked Iggy as he peeled what looked like a rotten banana off his shoulder.

"Calling you what?"

"Your Highness."

"Well, that's easy," snarled the captain. "Because you're a prince, Prince. And the last time I checked, a prince was royalty. And a commoner such as myself, when addressing someone of royalty such as yourself, must refer to you as Your Highness." The captain then bent down as a sign of respect. "If I had my hat, I would remove it, sir, but a most despicable dragon relieved me of it."

Iggy's stomach began to growl. He hadn't eaten any porridge all day and was very, very hungry. As he looked at the captain, who still had his head bowed before him, he began to wonder if this strange man with one leg might be crazy. He thought he should thank Captain Swell one more time for rescuing him and say good-bye. He would then go back inside the academy, sneak into the kitchen, and see if he could find some extra porridge to eat.

But when Iggy looked up at the tall dark towers of the academy, which appeared even more menacing in the dark night sky, a cold shiver ran through his body. He didn't want to go back inside, but then again, hanging around a strange man who thought he was a prince didn't seem like a good idea either.

Suddenly, the man with one leg slapped his left knee, straightened himself up, and pulled on the sides of his long coat, rather pleased with himself. "I must say, the others are going to be shocked that after so many years, it was I, Captain Bartholomew Swell, the hero of the battle over Fire Island, who finally found you, sir."

"CAWWW!" screeched the crow on the captain's shoulder.

"Okay. Okay. I wouldn't have found him without your help, Napoleon. Yes. Yes, very true. Now be quiet, or this won't be a successful rescue operation. Now let's get going."

The captain hobbled past Iggy toward a small wooden cart covered by a blanket. He raised the blanket and motioned to Iggy.

"In you go, Prince."

Iggy cautiously took a few steps back. He quickly glanced at the academy and then at the captain who stood by the cart.

"I'm dreaming," Iggy thought. "I must still be at the bottom of the well and dreaming because this is all a bunch of nonsense. I'm no prince. I'm Vomit Face. Fatso. Stinky Iggy. An idiot. A loser. Or if I'm not dreaming, this man with one leg and a crow for a friend is crazy. Who knows what he means to do with me? Maybe he's a cannibal and he wants to eat me for breakfast later this morning."

"Now, Prince, I really must insist that we get going, while it's still dark out," said the captain, cautiously looking around.

Frightened, Iggy turned and hurried toward

the academy. But then, all of a sudden, Iggy couldn't move. The captain had lassoed a rope around his waist! The rope tightened as Iggy fell to the ground and was dragged back toward the captain.

"Hey, let me go. Let me go!"

"I'm sorry, Prince. I don't fancy doing this. But I reckon it's for your own good."

Captain Swell lifted Iggy over his shoulder and carried him toward the wooden cart.

Before Iggy realized what was happening, the captain dropped him into the cart and quickly tied his hands to one of its posts. He was stuck! In a matter of minutes, Iggy had gone from being trapped at the bottom of a well to being tied to a wooden cart by a crazy man who insisted he was a prince.

"Hey, let me out of here! Untie these knots!" Iggy shouted.

"I'm mighty sorry, Your Highness," responded the captain. "I lost you once, and I don't plan on losing you again."

"You're crazy!" cried Iggy. Realizing he'd rather be miserable in a place like the academy than become some crazy man's prisoner, Iggy shouted at the top of his lungs: "Help! Help!"

"If you keep shouting like that, sir, you're going to wake somebody up," said the captain.

"That's the whole idea," shouted Iggy. "You're crazy! Help! Somebody, please, help!"

"I _am_ trying to help you; don't you see?" replied the captain.

"CAWWW! CAWWW!" screeched the crow.

"This is the loudest rescue mission ever attempted," muttered the captain.

"I'm no prince. I'm just Iggy, and you're trying to kidnap me. Help! Help!" cried Iggy as loud as he could.

Then Iggy noticed a candle flickering in one of the windows of the academy.

"I'm over here!" Iggy shouted when he saw the light.

The captain turned and looked up at the academy. He saw that the boy's screams had woken somebody up. He then looked at Iggy.

"I reckon you aren't leaving me much of a choice now, are you, Prince?" The captain sighed as he reached into his coat pocket and removed a red handkerchief. He took the handkerchief and covered Iggy's mouth. "This is just until we get out of here, Your Highness, so nobody can follow your screams. I promise. Now off we go."

The captain took the blanket and covered the cart, making sure Iggy could not be seen. In the darkness, Iggy tried to free his hands but couldn't. The crazy captain had tied too strong a knot. And now with his mouth covered, there was no way he could scream for help. Iggy then felt the wooden cart begin to roll. Where were they going?! What was going to happen to him?!

"Don't worry, Prince," the captain's gravelly voice whispered through the blanket. "Everything is going to be fine. You once were lost, but now you're found. And finally you can regain your throne."

Iggy grew more frightened. At least down at the bottom of the well he knew where he was. With this crazy man who thought he was a prince, there was no telling what might happen. What other oddities did this stranger believe? And more importantly, what exactly did he plan to do with him? As the cart rolled along, Iggy grew more and more frightened. And when he heard the sound of a gate smack shut, he realized his days at the academy might finally be over…but not how he had imagined.

## Chapter 6

In the king's study, King Naysayer wiggled impatiently in his chair. He watched as Mr. Winkle—his royal appraiser—peered through a glass magnifier, examin-ing a very tiny wooden ship encased in a glass bottle. The ship was a birthday present from King Frugal. King Naysayer wanted to know exactly how much it was worth. He firmly believed only an expensive present was worth giving.

"I don't have all day, Winkle. How much is that darn thing worth?"

"Almost there, Your Highness," said Mr. Winkle. The glass magnifier then plopped out of his eye and dropped into his hand. He quickly turned to a thick book resting on the king's desk and began flipping through its pages. When he found what he was looking for, he looked up from the book, and then back at the tiny wooden ship, then back at the book. With his eyes half closed, Mr. Winkle took a deep breath.

"Well?" asked the king.

Mr. Winkle took another deep breath. He closed

the book and placed it under his arm. He nervously looked at the king. "I'm afraid, Your Highness, the ship has a resale value of two duckets."

"Two duckets?! That's it?!" shouted the king as he swiped his arm across the desk and knocked the bottle containing the ship onto the floor. The glass casing surrounding the ship shattered into a million tiny pieces.

"Now it's probably worth a little less," said Mr. Winkle, sighing.

The king angrily plopped back into his chair and gave Mr. Winkle a cold stare.

"That cheapskate, King Frugal!" shouted the king. "He's lucky I don't start a war with him for sending me such a worthless birthday present! Wars have been started over a lot less, I promise you that! Let's see if he likes being treated with such disrespect. You know what I'm going to send him on his birthday? Do you, Mr. Winkle?"

Mr. Winkle shook his head slowly, side to side, indicating he did not.

"I'll send him a box!" shouted the king as a plan began forming in his vengeful mind. "And do you know what will be in that box?!"

Mr. Winkle did not reply. His eyes suddenly fixated on the bright red ring on the king's finger. The appraiser quickly leafed through his appraisal book once again.

"Nothing but sand!" proclaimed the king, very pleased by the trick he had just devised. "For his birthday, I'll send King Frugal a box full of nothing but worthless sand! What do you say to that, Winkle? How would you like to receive a box full of sand on your birthday? I bet you wouldn't like that at all! I bet, knowing your fragile disposition, you might even get depressed and cry about it. Well, that's what I hope happens to King Frugal. I hope he cries on his birthday because he's _so_ sad that all he got was a box full of sand. That will teach him not to send me a present that's only worth two lousy duckets! Mr. Winkle…are you even listening to me?!"

Mr. Winkle slammed his appraisal book shut. His mouth dropped open.

"Well, say something. Don't just stare at me like that. You look like a fool."

Mr. Winkle slowly raised his arm and pointed at the king's hand.

"Don't point your finger at me, Winkle. That's a criminal offense, and you know it."

"But—but…" stuttered Mr. Winkle.

"What's gotten into you, man?" said the king, annoyed.

"That—that—that ring…" Mr. Winkle finally managed to say.

King Naysayer looked at the ring he had taken from Iggy.

"Do you like it?" asked the king with a smirk. "I just got it this morning."

Mr. Winkle scrambled to the king's side and slid the appraisal book in front of him. King Naysayer peered down at the book and saw a drawing of the exact ring he wore on his finger. He read the description underneath the drawing:

"The Royal Rose Ring belongs to the Rose Kingdom and is worn by the ruler of the kingdom. The ring is known to have special powers when in the possession of its rightful heir. Approximate value: priceless."

Both Mr. Winkle and King Naysayer slowly turned and stared at each other, realizing the implications of what the king had just read.

"It's the Royal Rose Ring," whispered Mr. Winkle. "Priceless."

King Naysayer quickly jumped out of his chair, took Mr. Winkle by the hands, and began dancing with him around the room.

"Ha! I can't believe my luck!" shouted the king as he skipped gleefully with Mr. Winkle in tow.

"Excuse me, Your Highness, but how did you come into possession of such a wonderful birthday present?" asked Mr. Winkle.

The king suddenly froze. He sensed a realization was coming! He shoved Mr. Winkle to the floor and began pacing, his hands behind his back.

"That means that little twerp…" he muttered.

"I'm sorry…what, Your Highness?" asked Mr. Winkle as he got up from the ground.

"That means that little twerp," muttered King Naysayer to himself, "is ruler of the Rose Kingdom."

"But I thought Queen Victoria was ruler of the Rose Kingdom?" said Mr. Winkle.

"But maybe she's not the rightful ruler, you idiot!" snapped the king. He turned and faced Mr. Winkle. "Maybe that little boy…what was his name again? Maurice?…Kevin?…Vladimir?…No, that's not it…Iggy! That was it! Iggy! Iggy! Of course! That boy washed up on our shores in a basket when he was just a baby. Maybe somebody tried to smuggle him out of the kingdom for his own safety? The Rose Kingdom is halfway around the world… and he washed up here…" King Naysayer slowly realized the implications of what he had just said. He began jumping up and down in excitement.

The king was very out of shape, and all that jumping up and down quickly exhausted him. Struggling to catch his breath, he plodded back toward his desk and plopped back into his chair.

As the king wheezed and tried to catch his breath, Mr. Winkle walked over to the king's desk and picked up his appraisal book. "What do you think Queen Victoria will do when she discovers that you not only possess the Rose Ring, but you also know the whereabouts of the rightful heir to the throne?"

After a long stretch of time, the king finally regained his composure and spoke.

"As long as I have the boy and the ring, I think she'll do whatever I want her to." He began rubbing his hands together in eager anticipation. "I must immediately send word to Miss Spitfire to bring that boy Iggy to me. That little boy is going to make me very rich, Mr. Winkle. Very, very rich."

"That's great news, Your Highness," said Mr. Winkle. "Because we all know how much you love money."

# Chapter 7

In the early morning, while everyone in the Naysayer Academy was eating breakfast, Miss Spitfire peered down into the trash well. The nauseating stench forced her to cover her nose and mouth. Teddy, who was standing far behind her, yawned and wiped the sleep out of his eyes. Miss Spitfire had interrupted his breakfast, asking for Iggy's whereabouts. When he told her he had thrown Iggy down the trash well, she dragged him away from his bowl of porridge and demanded he show her exactly where.

"Am I going to get any extra credit for this, Miss Spitfire?" Teddy asked. "Or maybe an extra helping of porridge for lunch? It takes a lot of work coming up with new ways to torment Iggy. Sometimes I spend all night thinking up stuff."

Miss Spitfire squinted as she scanned the bottom of the trash well. All she saw was trash. No Iggy.

"Maybe you should consider giving me my own bedroom," continued Teddy, the thought pleasing him.

Miss Spitfire slowly leaned back and closed her eyes. She took a deep breath and walked away from the trash well and toward Teddy.

"You said you dropped him down the well. Is that right, Teddy?"

"Yep, right after school. Originally, I was thinking of hanging him upside down from the flagpole. But I did that last week. I don't like to repeat myself, you see. So, then I thought of the trash well. I figured I'd let him out later today, maybe after breakfast."

Miss Spitfire smacked her walking staff on the ground.

"If you say you dropped him down a twenty-foot well, then how come I don't see him down there?!"

Teddy quickly ran to the well and looked down. The stench almost made him throw up. He nervously turned around.

"But that's impossible; he's got to be down

there," he said. Miss Spitfire smacked him over the head with her walking stick.

"Ow!"

"Not <u>ow</u>, Teddy!" Miss Spitfire spat. "But <u>how</u>?! How did he get out of there?!"

"I—I—I don't know," said Teddy nervously as he took a few steps back. "I made sure the lid was on tight. There's no way he could have gotten all the way up without a rope or something. Somebody must have helped him get out."

"You said he doesn't have any friends!"

"He doesn't," said Teddy, rubbing the top of his head. "He's a loser."

Miss Spitfire then noticed some markings on the ground. She immediately bent over and began examining the dirt. She stopped when she clearly made out the tracks of a wheeled cart, followed by repeated markings of a man's boot. Miss Spitfire's eyes turned a bright shade of red. "Damn it!"

Teddy followed Miss Spitfire's tall body as she sprinted toward the front gate of the academy. His stomach dropped when he saw Miss Spitfire turn around, holding a broken lock in her hand. Teddy knew he was in trouble now.

"I—I—I'm sorry about this, Miss Spitfire," Teddy stammered. "I—I—I didn't think he had any friends. My plan was to make him spend the whole night down in the trash, and then I would let him out in the morning. That was the plan."

Miss Spitfire's red eyes burrowed into Teddy. "Well, your plan didn't work, did it, Teddy?!"

Then suddenly Miss Spitfire darted toward Teddy, grabbed him by the ear, and flung his large body into the air. Teddy landed on the ground a few feet from the old woman. He looked up and saw Miss Spitfire taking slow, calculated steps toward him. Her eyes were now a flaming bright red. He heard her knuckles crack as she tightened her grip on her walking staff. As Miss Spitfire moved closer, Teddy nervously crawled backward on his hands.

"I'm sorry. I'm so sorry, Miss Spitfire."

"Do you realize what you've let happen? Do you know how much trouble I'm in?!" the old woman hissed.

"I didn't mean to! I swear! I didn't think anybody would help him get out."

"He could be anywhere now. How am I going to deliver him to the king when I don't even know where he is?"

"I—I—I'll help you find him. I promise."

The old teacher hovered over Teddy. Teddy couldn't stand up. He was too frightened to move.

"If he leaves Naysayer, the king is going to put me in the Tower of Torture, Teddy. And I don't want to get tortured!"

"Neither do I!" cried Teddy.

"Who helped him escape?"

"I don't know! I swear. I'm so sorry!"

Miss Spitfire looked down at the frightened boy. She believed him, but that didn't matter. The only thing that mattered was finding Iggy and delivering him to the king. Because if she didn't, the king would make certain she was not only tortured upside down, but possibly even inside out. But Iggy could be anywhere. How was she going to find Iggy all by herself when he could be anywhere in the kingdom? More importantly, how was she going to conduct her search without making the king aware that Iggy had gone missing in the first place? Time was running out. She needed to act quickly.

Miss Spitfire pounded her walking staff on the ground, raised it into the air, and, with an exaggerated motion, pointed it straight at Teddy. A bright light shot from the wooden staff. The light blinded Teddy. It was burning hot. Teddy felt something strange happening, like there were a million spiders running all over his body. When he finally opened his eyes, he was shocked to see himself staring at Miss Spitfire's black pointy shoes. Her shoes were enormous! Teddy looked up, and in the far distance, he saw the old woman looking down at him. She was the size of a giant! What had she done to him?

Miss Spitfire bent down. Teddy saw her gigantic hand reach behind him and then slowly pull him up. Teddy tried to speak, but all he heard was a series of high-pitched squeaks. Miss Spitfire lifted him, so he was now able to stare into her face. In the reflection of her eyes, Teddy saw the most frightening sight. He saw the face of a white rat staring right back at him!

"If you find Iggy, then I'll turn you back to normal. But if you don't find him," warned Miss Spitfire, "you'll stay like this forever. Do you understand, Teddy?"

Teddy tried to protest, but again, all he managed were squeaks—one long one after another.

Realizing Teddy would need help, Miss Spitfire glanced toward the front entrance of the Naysayer Academy. She suddenly had a thought. Carrying Teddy by his long tail, she went back into the academy and sprinted toward the cafeteria. The children were horrified when Miss Spitfire surprised them during breakfast and turned each one of them into rats...just like Teddy. A few moments later, the front doors to the Naysayer Academy flung open, and an army of rats poured down the building's front steps. The rats scurried through the front gate and off into town, filling the morning air with loud squeaks as they began their search for Iggy.

After the last rat ran past her, Miss Spitfire slammed the academy's door shut and followed the children out the front gate. While they searched the kingdom for Iggy, Miss Spitfire had to see if she could buy herself some time with King Naysayer. She only hoped the king believed her lie.

# Chapter 8

Iggy tugged at the ropes that bound his hands to the inside post of the cart. They loosened slightly, but at this rate, it would take him forever to get free. Iggy wished he were stronger and bigger. He bet somebody like Teddy wouldn't have a problem getting out of this mess.

"I can't believe I just wished I was like Teddy," thought Iggy. "That's disgusting."

"Don't worry, Prince," Iggy heard the captain whisper through the blanket covering the cart. "Once we get you somewhere safe, I'll untie you and we can have some of that delicious wombat stew."

Iggy looked at the small black pot at the other end of the cart. So, that was causing the smell. This whole time Iggy thought it was him. He had never heard of wombat stew, but the nauseating smell from the pot did not entice him to try it. He'd rather have porridge any day of the week. Since the captain's handkerchief was still firmly covering his mouth, Iggy could merely grunt in protest.

"Aye, I do regret having to put you in this position, Prince, but you got to trust me. It's for your own good. And after we get a little wombat in your belly, I reckon you'll be in a much better disposition. Or at least I hope so."

"The minute you untie me, I'm running. I don't know where to, but as far away from you as I can. And stop calling me Prince," Iggy cried. But to the captain it simply sounded like repeated grunting. Iggy tugged harder at the ropes and twisted his body this way and that.

"I do wish you would keep still, Your Highness," pleaded the captain, "or else all these Naysayers are going to start wondering what's in my cart."

"That's the idea," Iggy wanted to cry out.

He finally managed to loosen the ropes a little more and was able to peek out from underneath the blanket covering the cart. In the distance, he saw a shipyard bustling with activity. And as the cart bumped along in the morning light, Iggy watched men unload heavy crates from large wooden ships. The sounds of shouting and cackling and squeaking filled the morning air. The biggest men Iggy had ever seen—even bigger than Teddy—carried wooden crates filled with pigs, chickens, and monkeys. Then Iggy's eyes nearly popped out of his head when he saw a gigantic white elephant being lowered onto the dock. He watched all this with wonder. He had never been outside the academy before, and although he had heard of monkeys and chickens and elephants, he had never actually seen any with his own two eyes. For a brief moment, Iggy was in such awe that he completely forgot he had been kidnapped. But that quickly changed when he realized the captain was rolling the wooden cart behind a wall of empty crates, in a deserted part of the shipyard.

"This looks like a good place," said the captain, as he pulled the blanket off the cart and smiled down at Iggy. "Now how about some wombat stew? I don't know about you, but I'm as hungry as an ox."

The captain removed the handkerchief from Iggy's mouth. He began to untie the rope around his hands when they both heard somebody behind them say: "Well, look what we got here."

"Not a word, Prince. Keep very quiet," said the captain as he quickly threw the blanket back over him.

"What now?" Iggy muttered, rather annoyed.

"Looks like we got ourselves a bum," he heard a man say in a very menacing tone.

"A really ugly looking one too," said another man.

For a second, Iggy thought these men might be able to help him, but the tone in their voices reminded him of Teddy's voice, just before he was about to beat him up.

"Aye, mates, I reckon I don't want any trouble,"

Iggy heard the captain say. "Me and my crow are just on our way home."

The strangers laughed.

"Home, and where's that? Sleeping in the gutter!" one of the men shouted. Iggy was getting scared. "This captain may be crazy," he thought, "but these men sound like trouble."

"What's inside the cart, bum?" one of men asked.

"Inside the cart?" repeated the captain. "Why, nothing that would interest three buffoons like yourselves." The captain lifted the blanket and winked at Iggy. "Let's see, just a Guzzlebeery's horn, a rainbow, and a coat made of ice." He lowered the blanket back down. "Like I said, nothing that would interest three knuckleheads."

"Hey, he's lying," Iggy heard one of the men say. "There ain't such a thing as a coat made of ice. And I don't think a rainbow could fit in a cart either."

"Aye, shows how much you know," sneered the captain.

"You sure you don't have anything of _real_ value in that cart of yours? Like some duckets? Times are tough these days. You know what I'm saying?"

Iggy didn't move a muscle. He then heard the captain growl, "Aye, I'm quite sure I have nothing that would interest three fine ingrates like yourselves. And I reckon you wouldn't know something of _real_ value if it bit you on your arse!"

"Is that so?" one of the men sneered. "Well, why don't we just take a look for ourselves."

Iggy heard the sound of footsteps getting closer.

"I don't think so," snorted the captain.

"I think you're forgetting something, bum."

"Aye, what's that?" grunted the captain.

"It's three against one."

Iggy then heard a thunderous laugh. "Just shows how much you know," he heard the captain say. "Why, I've wrestled dragons to the bottom of the ocean floor! I've tussled on a Nickleberry's back! I've even dropped down into the Murdoch Pits of Fire, just because I was bored! Three against one?! Ha!" barked the captain. "You're the ones who should be worried!"

Suddenly, Iggy heard a loud CRACK! A fight had broken out! Huddled underneath the blanket, he listened to the loud smack of punches being thrown and the harsh thud of kicks. Then Iggy heard a loud crashing sound, followed by a bunch of OWWS and GRUNTS. It sounded like the captain was kicking butt!

Iggy had to see it for himself. He couldn't keep hidden any longer. He raised his head and peered out from underneath the blanket. He couldn't believe what he saw! He had gotten it all wrong. The captain wasn't kicking butt, but was getting his butt kicked! And properly too!

Three men surrounded the captain, each taking turns kicking him in the stomach and punching him in the face. One smashed a wooden crate over his head. Then things got particularly ugly. One of the men, the smallest of the three, grabbed the captain's wooden leg and pulled it off. The other men laughed as their small partner began twirling it around. Then he threw it up into the air. Iggy watched as the captain's wooden leg bounced onto the dock and landed not very far from the wooden cart.

"You took my leg! That ain't fair!" growled the captain as he took another punch to the face.

"Fair," shouted the short man again. "Life ain't

fair!" Then all three men kicked the captain over and over again.

Iggy couldn't stand the sight of it any longer. He dropped back into the cart and covered his ears and closed his eyes. What if after beating up the captain, the men found him in the cart? What would they do to him? They'd probably give him a more painful beating than he ever got from Teddy…or maybe even something worse. Iggy had to get away. If he hurried, the men might not even notice him because they were too busy beating up the captain. Iggy raised his head and nervously peered over the cart. He saw another wall of empty crates at the far end of the dock. If he ran fast enough, he could sneak behind one of those crates until he felt it was safe. But he had to make a run for it right now, while the men weren't looking. It was now or never.

Iggy took a deep breath and jumped out of the cart. He ran toward the other wall of crates. But after running only a few feet, he suddenly stopped, when he saw the captain's wooden leg.

Iggy then turned around. He watched as the captain, now helpless, took several punches to his face and kicks to his stomach. Napoleon, the crow, was flying high above them all, CAWWING at the men as he tried to poke at their heads.

Iggy was reminded of all the times he had been

beaten up at the academy. How all the children would gather in a circle and cheer as Teddy kicked him in the stomach or punched him in the face; how he would lie there, hoping that this beating didn't last as long as the last one; how he would lie on the ground, listening to the children scream in his ears, and hope that just one of the kids, just one, would tell the rest to stop. No one ever did. Maybe the grown men who were now beating up the captain were former students of the academy. Maybe, just like Teddy, when they were children, they used to pick on boys smaller than them. Maybe they used to pick on boys just like him.

Iggy felt something happening inside him. His heart began racing. His fists suddenly clenched. His eyes became two perfect slits. He was angry.

"LEAVE HIM ALONE!" Iggy suddenly shouted at the top of his lungs. The three men stopped beating up the captain and turned to face him. What had he done?! There was no turning back now. Iggy bent down, picked up the captain's wooden leg, and clutched it in his hands. He felt his heart pounding louder in his chest. He was scared, but he was not going to run. He suddenly charged toward the three men and whacked each one of them with a good solid hit. He knocked one man on the head, another in the leg, and then the third on the back. He kept hitting and hitting and hitting! Napoleon the crow tried to peck out the men's eyes as all three stumbled backward, approaching the edge of the dock.

"Leave us alone," one of the men cried. And then, with one solid hit from the captain's wooden leg, Iggy knocked the shortest man off the dock. The man plunged into the water down below. Meanwhile, Napoleon pecked at the tallest man's head, until the man couldn't take it anymore and jumped off the dock, joining his partner in the water.

There was only one man left. Iggy raised the captain's wooden leg high above his head. He darted toward the man, yelling the whole way. The man decided he didn't want to get hit anymore and voluntarily jumped off the pier. Iggy leaned over the dock and watched as the three men swam away.

One of the men shouted as he looked up. "We got beaten up by a kid! That's just embarrassing!"

Napoleon landed on Iggy's shoulder and let out a loud "CAWWW!"

Iggy struggled to catch his breath. He then turned away from the sea and walked over to the captain, who was having difficulty getting up.

"Are you okay?"

The captain's face was swollen, and he appeared to be in quite a bit of pain.

"Aye, I'll be all right," muttered the captain, struggling to balance himself on his one good leg. "Aye, Prince, you fancy giving me back my leg? I don't feel quite myself without it."

Iggy handed the captain his wooden leg and helped him put it on. With his leg back in place, the captain straightened his coat and tried to stand tall. Napoleon flew off of Iggy and landed back on the captain's shoulder.

"Aye, if they hadn't taken my leg, it would have been a fair fight. Why, in my younger days, I fought a three-headed dragon off the shores of Lingus, all with nothing but a teacup." The captain then sighed deeply. "Ah, those were the days. Now I'm a shadow of my former self."

There was a moment of silence. Iggy watched as the captain looked down at the ground, his face not only bruised from the fight but also looking very sad. Napoleon then squawked.

"Aye, I guess you're right, Napoleon," muttered the captain.

The captain turned to face Iggy and extended his hand.

"Thank you, Prince, for all your help."

Iggy peered up at the captain, whose eyes were getting swollen, and shook his hand.

"No problem."

"Now how about some wombat stew?" asked the captain.

Iggy couldn't believe it, but he actually agreed.

As they both made their way back to the wooden cart, Iggy noticed that the captain's swollen face was turning black and blue.

"Does it hurt?"

The captain laughed. "No pain, no gain, my prince. Besides, you can't call yourself a man of action without getting a few bruises, can you?"

The captain reached into the cart and took out the pot. "This here is the best wombat stew this side of the Crystal Ocean," he said, as he lifted the lid off the pot and inhaled deeply. "And, may I add, is my mum's very own recipe."

Iggy nervously smiled as the stench from the stew began to make his stomach turn upside down.

Years later, when Iggy remembered that moment with the captain, he would often smile. It was the first time he felt he had a friend.

# Chapter 9

Outside the king's chambers, Miss Spitfire nervously paced back and forth until the guard, a large green ogre with flaring nostrils, returned. He growled—as ogres are prone to do—and told her the king would finally see her. When she asked the guard if the king was in a good mood, the ogre growled once again and said, "Yes, surprisingly. He says this birthday is going to be his best ever."

"Well, that's wonderful," said Miss Spitfire, secretly more worried than ever.

When they entered the king's chamber—a large, ornate room—Miss Spitfire's eyes widened at the sight of the short, plump king reclining in a golden chair. Several servants surrounded him. Some servants filed his toenails, while others massaged his short, pudgy white hands; one plucked his eyebrows, while another trimmed his tiny mustache.

"Do you realize what a wonderful day it is, Miss Spitfire?" gleefully shouted the king when he saw the old woman standing before him.

"Wonderful? Oh yes, quite wonderful, Your Highness," said Miss Spitfire as she nervously bowed her head.

"My birthday is only a day away," continued the king, "and _you_, of all people, have surprised me with the best present ever." The king admired the Rose Ring on his pudgy finger.

"Well, isn't that just…just wonderful," said Miss Spitfire as her mouth grew dry.

"Speaking of which," said the king with delight, "where is he? Is he hiding behind you?"

"Oh…no…no, Your Highness…not behind me, I'm afraid," said Miss Spitfire as she forced a grin. "He's…uh…he's on a class trip, Your Majesty."

The king's eyes suddenly narrowed. Miss Spitfire took an immediate step back.

"A class trip?" said the king coldly.

"Yes, Your Highness," said Miss Spitfire as she tightly gripped her walking staff. "You see, Your Majesty, since the kids did such a wonderful job yesterday when you came to visit, I rewarded them with a class trip."

"We're not supposed to reward children, but punish them," said the king, the smile on his face now gone and replaced with a scowl.

"True, Your Highness, but wait until I tell you the class trip I sent them on," said Miss Spitfire as she prepared to lie to the king. "You see, Your Majesty, I had Iggy and his classmates visit the Tower of Torture, so they could see all the wonderful new torture techniques you invented."

The king sighed and closed his eyes.

"After all," nervously continued Miss Spitfire, "the best way to make sure kids turn out the way we want them to is by showing them the punishment they'll receive if they don't obey." Miss Spitfire then forced an awkward smile, hoping for her dear life that the king believed her lie.

But as one of his servants plucked another hair from his eyebrow, the king sank lower into his chair, wrapping his knuckles around the armrests. He then opened his eyes and fixed an angry stare on the school headmistress. After what felt like an eternity, the king finally spoke.

"Since you are so interested in showing the students some of my new torture techniques, do you know, Miss Spitfire, what some of them are?"

Miss Spitfire slowly shook her head no.

"Can any of you help Miss Spitfire?" the king asked his servants.

The woman plucking his eyebrows stopped and said, "You get hung upside down and tickled to death."

"What else?" asked the king.

"You get covered in honey and attacked by bees," said the man filing the king's toenails.

"What else?" asked the king.

"You have to eat twenty jars of peanut butter without having a glass of water," said the woman trimming the king's nose hair.

"That's one of my favorites. What else?" asked the king.

"You have to spin around in one spot until you get sick at least twenty times," said another servant.

Suddenly Miss Spitfire burst into tears.

"Now, Miss Spitfire," said the king, very calmly, "what is the first rule as head of the Naysayer Academy that you are absolutely, under no condition, ever to break?"

Miss Spitfire sobbed deeply. "I'm never supposed to let the children out of the academy. I'm so sorry, Your Majesty. I don't know where Iggy is. He's escaped. One of the boys dropped him down our trash well, but this morning when I went to look for him, he was gone. Please don't make me eat twenty jars of peanut butter. I'm allergic to peanut butter!!"

The king closed his eyes and sighed. He then waved away his servants. "Leave us."

The king bounced out off his chair and walked over to Miss Spitfire. He slowly smiled. Miss Spitfire looked into the king's dark eyes and saw her scared reflection. She quickly looked away, continuing to cry. The king offered her a handkerchief as he led her by the arm. Her hands shaking, Miss Spitfire took the handkerchief and blew her nose. She was so upset, she didn't realize the king was leading her toward the balcony outside his room.

"Do you know why I asked you to become headmistress of the Naysayer Academy, all those years ago?" said the king, as they approached the edge of the balcony.

Miss Spitfire blew her nose once again.

"You said I was the meanest person you had ever met, except for you, of course, Your Majesty."

"That's right. You had so much potential."

Then Miss Spitfire realized what was about to happen. When she turned, the king had her firmly in his grasp. Suddenly he lifted her off the ground. With lightning speed, the king turned Miss Spitfire upside down and hung her over the balcony by her feet. Miss Spitfire gasped as she looked at the kingdom of Naysayer below her. She squeezed her eyes shut. Deathly afraid of heights, she gripped her walking staff with all her might. She prayed the king wouldn't drop her.

"No, Your Majesty, please!" shouted Miss Spitfire.

"That kid Iggy was the best birthday present I ever got!!!" shouted the king, as he shook Miss Spitfire up and down.

"But I don't understand, Your Majesty. He's a loser. Nobody likes him!!" Miss Spitfire cried as she felt the blood rush to her head.

"He's prince of the Rose Kingdom," shouted the king as he continued shaking Miss Spitfire. "He's worth a fortune! Queen Victoria will offer me all the money in the world to keep his existence a secret. And you know how much I love money!"

"Iggy…a prince, but that's impossible!" Miss Spitfire shouted as she felt herself getting dizzy.

"Impossible, but true," said the king, as he grew tired and struggled to lift Miss Spitfire back onto the balcony.

Miss Spitfire took a deep breath in relief, her bony knees still shaking. The king shoved his hand in front of the headmistress and pointed to the Rose Ring.

"This ring belongs to the prince of the Rose Kingdom," wheezed the king, as he tried to catch his breath. "That boy Iggy washed up on our shores ten years ago. This ring was wrapped around his finger, and we never made the connection."

"Well, the Rose Kingdom is very far away…" said Miss Spitfire as she held on to the balcony railing to regain her balance.

"That might be…But now that we know the truth about Iggy, you let him escape from the academy."

"Your Highness, I am doing my best to locate him. I've turned all the children into rats. They are searching the kingdom for him, as we speak."

"Why rats? Why not a flock of birds, so they could fly around the kingdom? Birds would have a much better chance of finding him than an army of rats."

"True," said Miss Spitfire, as she pinned her gray hair back in place. "But, unfortunately, this magic staff only lets me transform children into rats. That's it. Nothing but rats."

The king walked back into his royal chamber and sank into his chair.

"I didn't drop you, Miss Spitfire, because I expect you to find the boy and bring him to me."

"I will, Your Majesty." Miss Spitfire walked back into the room and bowed before the king. "Thank you for your forgiving mood."

"If you don't find the boy," said the king, "I will only have you to blame. You will have ruined my birthday, and you know how much I love my birthday."

"Yes, yes, I do," said Miss Spitfire.

The king stared at the old woman bowing before him. "If you fail to find this boy, which punishment do you prefer? Being tarred and feathered? Or hung by your toes while crows peck out your eyes?"

Miss Spitfire let out a deep hiss. Neither option sounded appealing. "Don't worry, Your Highness. I'll find him."

"You better!" shouted the king. "Now get to it!"

Miss Spitfire quickly darted out of the room as the king sank deeper into his chair.

# Chapter 10

**M**any years ago, in the Rose Kingdom, King Rose lay in bed. He held a newborn baby boy in his arms. Through labored breaths he spoke. "I'm dying, my son. My sister has seen to that."

The baby boy looked up at the old man with a gray beard and smiled, blissfully unaware of the turn his life was about to take.

"I want you to remember, no matter what happens, you are not alone. I will always love you." The king tried to catch his breath. He rested the child on his lap and removed a silver ring with a bright red stone from his finger. The red stone shone brightly. The king then gently raised the baby's tiny hand and slid the large ring onto his son's finger. Magically the ring shrank in size to fit the baby's finger. The baby marveled at the ring and giggled as it caught a ray of moonlight and sparkled.

There was a knock at the door.

"Enter," said the king in the loudest whisper he could muster.

Four people entered the room and hurried to the edge of the king's bed. The sight of their ruler so frail, so inexplicably old, took them by surprise.

"My king," said a man with one leg. "What has happened? You've gone from a man of thirty to a man of ninety in not even a fortnight."

The king looked at his faithful servant Captain Swell.

"My sister wishes me dead," said the king. "She made sure my wife would not survive childbirth. And now, through a spell, she has seen to it that I will age so quickly that I won't live to see my own son grow up."

"Perhaps I can reverse the spell," said a young woman with raven-black hair. She came to the king's side.

"I fear this magic is too strong, even for someone as gifted as you, Miss Blackfeather," sighed the king.

"Well, we have to do something. We can't let you die, Your Majesty," protested a young man with wavy long hair. "Professor, can't your science do something to help him?" said the young man to a tall bald man at his side.

"I would first have to know what I'm dealing with," said the bald man as he removed his wire-framed glasses and came to the edge of the bed. "I'd have to run tests and diagnose—"

"There's no time!" the king shouted, and then labored to catch his breath. After a long silence, in which the king finally stopped wheezing, he continued to speak at a more measured pace. "I asked you here to sneak my son out of the kingdom. I fear my sister wants him dead, so she has no challenge to the throne."

"Aye, Your Highness. Where should we take him?" asked Captain Swell.

"To the kingdom of Crystal. Queen Prism will provide you all with safe quarters until he is old enough to regain his throne. Now, you must hurry, before my sister, Victoria, realizes what has happened."

The servants all bowed. The king then lifted the baby. Miss Blackfeather carefully took the boy in her arms.

"You are my most faithful servants. I trust you with my child. I want him to learn from you all that is good and right."

The servants bowed once more, then kissed their king on the hand and quietly left with the child. Once they had gone, the king fell back into bed, closed his eyes, and listened to his breath, wondering which one would be his last. He prayed that his son made it safely out of the kingdom.

Later that night, the four servants took the child and snuck him onto the captain's ship, the *Lucky Rose*. The next morning, when Victoria—the king's sister—visited the king to make sure he was dying as planned, she realized the baby boy had disappeared.

"You shouldn't have done that, Your Majesty," whispered Victoria into the king's ear.

"He's the heir to the throne: not you," said the king, coughing.

"He can't be the heir to the throne if he dies at sea!" shouted Victoria as she stormed out of the room.

* * *

Later that day, while the king's trusted servants were out at sea, Miss Blackfeather watched as dark thunderclouds floated across the bright blue sky toward them. She gripped the wicker basket holding the baby boy.

"I think Victoria is onto us," she shouted to the others, pointing to the approaching storm.

"You better hold on to something," shouted Captain Swell as he tried to navigate his ship, the *Lucky Rose*, away from the clouds. But the ship couldn't sail fast enough, and it was soon caught in the grip of the most violent storm any of them had ever encountered. The ship bounced up and down, crashing from wave to wave. The brutal rain cut through the ship's sails. Then suddenly a thunderbolt hit the masthead, cracking the wood, and the *Lucky Rose* began to spin wildly out of control.

The baby started to cry, frightened by the sound of thunder. Miss Blackfeather tightened her grip on the wicker basket, scrambling to find something to hold on to as wave upon wave crashed against the ship. Then, without warning, an enormous wave crashed onto the deck and heaved Miss Blackfeather overboard. Miss Blackfeather tumbled and tossed under the water. When she finally came up for air, she looked around frantically. The basket was missing.

## Chapter 11

Captain Swell let out a gigantic burp. Iggy looked at him with disbelief, a spoonful of wombat stew dangling from his hand.

"So I just floated out to sea?" asked Iggy.

"I reckon so," said the captain as he wiped his mouth with a handkerchief. "Once the storm passed, we all swam for what seemed like an eternity, until we landed on a small island. We built a small raft and went looking for you. We searched for years, never wanting to give up hope, but then eventually I guess we did just that. I mean, what do you reckon are the chances of a newborn baby floating safely out of a hurricane in nothing but a wicker basket? I ain't as smart as Professor Jones, but I reckon that chances are not high."

"So, what happened after you gave up looking for me?"

"What happened? What happened?" repeated the captain. He then spoke softly. "Well, a dark cloud, worse than the one from that hurricane, came over us. We had failed in our duty. We had not only let your father down, our beloved king, but also the people of the Rose Kingdom. A miserable lot the four of us became. And after years of looking for you, eventually our misery led us here to the kingdom of Naysayer. I guess if you're going be miserable, there ain't no better place than here. Like Henry O'Henry always says: misery likes company."

"Where are the others?" Iggy asked.

"Once we got here, we went our separate ways." The captain sighed. "We couldn't stand being with each other anymore, because it was a reminder of how we had failed."

"CAWWW!!!" crowed Napoleon.

"That's right, Napoleon," said the captain, lightening up in spirit. "Then one day, while I was sitting here on this very dock, feeling very sorry for myself, wondering what was what, Napoleon flew onto my shoulder and told me he had found you. And now everything has changed. You better finish up that stew, Prince, so we can go and tell the others."

Iggy looked down at his spoon. Surprisingly, although it smelled like rotten toes, the wombat stew was actually quite delicious. Iggy had another helping of stew and pondered everything the captain had just told him. It made his head swirl. Was he really a long-lost prince? He didn't feel like a prince, but then again he wasn't sure how a prince was supposed to feel.

"Ready?" asked the captain as he stood and lifted the blanket over the cart. "We got to keep you hidden, Prince, until the others and I can figure out how to get you out of here."

Iggy slowly crept back into the cart, and the captain lowered the blanket. In the darkness Iggy felt the cart begin to roll, and then he heard the captain whisper, "The others won't believe it, Your Highness, that after all these years, after so much despair, we finally found you. It's a miracle."

"A miracle…" Iggy thought to himself. "Imagine that…me….stinky Iggy…being a miracle."

# Chapter 12

The wooden cart came to a stop. The captain lifted the blanket, and Iggy saw a small store window with red curtains in front of him. A sign above the store window read: Miss Blackfeather— Fortune-Teller.

"Now, Your Majesty, I think it best if you go and meet Miss Blackfeather by yourself."

Iggy noticed a door marked: Enter and Discover Your Future. "Why do I have to go alone?" he asked.

"Well, you see, Prince, Miss Blackfeather and I got into a bit of a disagreement a while back, and she might not be all that happy to see me."

"What kind of disagreement?"

"CAWWW!" crowed Napoleon.

"Napoleon, I am not acting like a baby," protested the captain. "You know how hard it is to find a hat that perfectly fits my head. And that witch just lit it on fire, without a care in the world."

"CAWWW!" crowed Napoleon again.

"Well, of course she's going to say it was an accident."

"I thought you said a dragon stole your hat," said Iggy.

"That was _another_ hat. You see, Prince, since Miss Blackfeather intentionally lit my favorite captain's hat on fire, I've had an awful string of bad luck. So terrible that I now refuse to even wear a hat, because every time I get a new hat, something awful happens to it _and_ me. That's why, Prince, I think it best if you see Miss Blackfeather on your own."

"What should I tell her?"

"Why, tell her the truth," said the captain. "Tell her you're Prince Rose of the Rose Kingdom."

# Chapter 13

Iggy slowly opened the door. He froze when he heard a bell jingle over his head. He saw red curtains in front of him, nervously parted them, and stepped into a small room. The room was lit with several candles. A multitude of different-colored jars rested on shelves lining the walls. Some jars had eyeballs in them; others had chicken claws. And on closer inspection, Iggy was shocked to see a green-colored jar containing a man's shrunken head.

"HISSSSSSS!"

Iggy jumped at the sound and saw a sleek black cat with bright yellow eyes staring at him. Suddenly, a curtain behind the cat parted, and a middle-aged woman with pale white skin and long black hair entered the room. The woman's arms were covered with tattoos, and her ears were pierced more times than Iggy thought humanly possible.

"That's the head of the chief of the Hooboola tribe. Cost me a fortune to get it, but I think it's a fake. It's supposed to help increase your hunger, or so they say. Though I've never managed to get the spell to work."

Iggy looked at the green jar and wondered how a small, shriveled-up head was supposed to make someone hungry.

He then noticed the woman looking at him suspiciously. "What are you doing here?" she said in a husky voice. "No kids allowed."

Iggy swallowed as the woman's bright, piercing blue eyes stared him up and down. "Are you Miss Blackfeather?"

"That's what it says on the sign, kid. Now, I repeat, no kids allowed in my store."

"Well, I have something to tell you."

"And what's that?" she asked, rather annoyed.

"I—I—I—" Iggy couldn't get the words out. Maybe because he was having such a hard time believing what he was trying to say.

"Out with it!" snapped Miss Blackfeather. "I don't have all day. I—I—I…"

"I'm Prince Iggy Rose of the Rose Kingdom," Iggy blurted out.

Silence. There, he'd said it, no matter how foolish it sounded. Miss Blackfeather stared at him with a blank expression. Then suddenly, she brushed past him and took a seat at a small round table. She crossed her legs and began shuffling through a deck of cards.

"I don't know who put you up to this, kid," she finally said. "But you better get out of here, before I turn you into a toad or a warthog."

Iggy swallowed hard. "Can you do that?"

"In theory, yes," snapped Miss Blackfeather. But then she looked at him and sighed. "But lately, I can't spin a spell to save my life. It must be all the negative energy in this blasted kingdom. Yesterday I tried to turn a flea into a dragon, and you know what the flea did?"

"No," answered Iggy.

"It spit in my eye and then walked away," she said in disbelief.

Iggy was shocked to hear himself chuckle.

"It's no laughing matter," said Miss Blackfeather very sternly.

Iggy's face froze.

"Without my magic who am I?" she said sadly. Iggy watched as Miss Blackfeather sighed and then slowly continued shuffling her deck of cards. "Listen, kid, like I said, I don't know who put you up to this, but I don't appreciate it. Just leave me alone."

"But the captain—" Iggy began to say.

"The captain!" barked Miss Blackfeather. "So that's who told you to come in here and say you're Prince Rose. Well, you tell that captain I'm sorry I accidentally lit his hat on fire. But that's no reason to play with a woman's emotions. Now leave me alone."

Iggy didn't know what to do. He watched as Miss Blackfeather forcefully shuffled through her deck of cards, visibly upset. He slowly walked over to the table.

Miss Blackfeather looked up at him.

"What do those cards do?" Iggy asked.

"They tell your fortune."

Iggy stood silent for a moment, noticing the strange drawings that decorated the face of the cards. One drawing was of a woman with two long swords; another, of a fire-breathing dragon. Then Iggy noticed a drawing of a dark hooded figure.

"Do you really believe that?" Iggy asked, finding it hard to understand how a simple deck of cards could tell somebody's whole life story.

"Hah," barked Miss Blackfeather. "You just sounded like the professor. Yes, I do believe it. There are things in this world that can't be explained. There's mystery all around us, kid. The sooner you accept it, the better off you'll be. Now, like I said before, leave!"

Miss Blackfeather gave him a sharp look, but Iggy didn't move. He couldn't leave without knowing the truth. He suddenly took a seat in the chair opposite her.

Miss Blackfeather rolled her eyes. "What are you doing? What part of _leave_ don't you understand?"

"If I'm really Prince Rose," Iggy quickly said, "then those cards should say it or show it, right?"

"I don't have time…" began Miss Blackfeather.

"Please," Iggy begged. "I don't know if I believe it either, but the captain says I am, and I just want to know if it's true. If I'm not, I'll leave you alone; I promise."

Miss Blackfeather stared at the boy. Iggy looked down.

"Please," he said softly. "It would be great to be anything other than Stinky Iggy or Vomit Face or Fathead—which, by the way, doesn't make any sense, because I see kids with a lot bigger heads than mine."

"Is that what the other kids call you?" asked Miss Blackfeather.

"Yeah," said Iggy as he looked at the shelves of colored jars, trying to avoid Miss Blackfeather's gaze. He didn't like talking about how the kids at the academy picked on him.

"Kids can be mean sometimes," Miss Blackfeather said softly. "And so can adults."

"Trust me, I know," said Iggy. He turned and faced Miss Blackfeather again. "Please, I just want to know, for me, if it's true."

Miss Blackfeather took a deep breath and looked at the young boy sitting across from her. "Now listen, kid," she began. "Don't get your hopes up here. Just because you're not the prince doesn't mean you're what all those other kids say you are. You are who you want to be. It all starts with what's in your heart, and in your head. You understand?"

Iggy nodded.

"Okay, then." Miss Blackfeather began to shuffle the cards again. "I just don't want you to get all sad on me. And, I don't appreciate the captain putting you up to this, but you seem like a nice kid…"

Miss Blackfeather closed her eyes and removed a card from the deck. She placed it on the table. She opened her eyes and looked down. The image of a blazing red star suddenly flashed through her mind. "But that's imposs…" she began to say.

"What's impossible?" asked Iggy, as he looked down at a card with a picture of a starry night sky.

Miss Blackfeather then put down another card. This one was decorated with the drawing of a bright golden crown. Iggy watched as Miss Blackfeather

closed her eyes and took a deep breath. She slowly drew another card from the deck. She placed it on the table. She peeked through one eye down at the card. Then she dropped the deck of cards, gasped, and covered her mouth.

"What is it?" asked Iggy as he looked at the card. He saw the drawing of an old man with a long white beard. Iggy looked up. Miss Blackfeather was staring straight at him, her eyes filled with tears. She reached over the table and pulled Iggy into her arms. She whispered softly in his ear.

"I thought I would never find you again. I lost all hope."

# Chapter 14

Professor Jones sighed heavily as he stared at the various springs and gears of a broken clock on his desk. He removed his glasses and began scratching his bald head. By his calculation, this would be the 1,534,222nd clock he had fixed this year. "How had this happened?" Professor Jones wondered to himself. "How did I go from creating time machines and robots and space rockets and mathematical formulas <u>so</u> complicated that only *I* could understand them to fixing broken clocks and toasters? Hadn't I discovered the formula for turning broccoli into scoops of chocolate ice cream? And if I hadn't accidentally blown up my laboratory, I would have probably discovered the formula for turning smelly old shoes into raspberry sorbet as well. Yes, without question, I'm a brilliant scientist. So why am I spending all my days fixing broken down clocks and toasters for the people of Naysayer?"

Professor Jones sighed again. Then with a swipe of his arm, he knocked the springs and gears of the broken clock onto the floor. "What's the point?" Professor Jones muttered. "These Naysayers don't really understand time anyway."

The professor reached into his pocket. He removed a flyer several of the king's men were handing out in Naysayer's main square that morning. He put his glasses back on and peered down at the paper. The flyer showed a drawing of a young boy. Under the boy's face, it read: KING NAYSAYER OFFERS 1 MILLION DUCKETS FOR THE SAFE CAPTURE AND DELIVERANCE OF THIS UGLY BOY.

The professor scratched his head again. One million duckets would provide him with the money he needed to fund his experiments. With that much money, he could build a rocket. Fly out of the kingdom of Naysayer and visit a far-off galaxy. Or, better yet, he could build another time machine and visit a whole other dimension. If he could find this boy, he could escape all of Naysayer's negative energy and go back to being the brilliant scientist he knew he was. Because the truth was, after arriving in Naysayer, Professor Jones had noticed his mental capacity diminishing with each passing day. He had to get out of Naysayer quickly, before his brain turned to mush. Realizing he didn't have a moment to lose, the professor slid open his desk drawer, removed a pencil and paper, and began calculating all the places in the kingdom the boy could be hiding. He stopped when the bell to his front door jingled. Somebody had entered his shop.

"I won't fix another clock or toaster as long as I live, so just go away!" shouted the professor.

"Well, I see your people skills haven't improved much," he heard a husky woman's voice say.

"It's because he spends too much time in his head and doesn't get enough exercise," he then heard a man snarl.

Professor Jones looked up and saw Miss Blackfeather and Captain Bartholomew Swell standing in his tiny repair shop. He quickly stood up, his bald head nearly touching the ceiling.

"What do you two want? I thought we agreed, when we washed up on these shores, that we would never speak to each other again?"

"Something's changed," said Miss Blackfeather. She and Captain Swell stepped aside and revealed Iggy standing behind them.

Professor Jones's mouth dropped open. He grabbed the flyer from his desk and looked down at the drawing of the young boy. He compared it to the young boy standing in his repair shop. It was the same boy!

Slightly annoyed, the professor said, "I suppose this means you two want to split the reward three ways, doesn't it?"

"What's he talking about?" asked Iggy, looking up at the captain and Miss Blackfeather.

Professor Jones handed the flyer over to the captain. The captain frowned when he saw the image of Iggy and the reward. He handed the flyer to Miss Blackfeather, who had the same reaction. She then slowly handed Iggy the flyer. Iggy looked down at the drawing of his face, which in his opinion wasn't very good but looked vaguely like him. He saw the reward being offered for his capture.

"A million duckets? Is that a lot?" asked Iggy as he looked back up at the captain and Miss Blackfeather.

"Is that a lot?!" said the professor, surprised. "Do you know what I could do with a million duckets?! I could build a rocket or a time machine or a gigantic robot. You name it, and I could build it. I'd finally have the money to put my intellect to good use and stop fixing these stupid clocks and toasters!"

"Does that mean you're going to hand me over to the king?" asked Iggy nervously.

"You bet we are," said the professor. "I thought it would take me at least a week to find you, but lucky for me, you showed up right on my doorstep."

The captain quickly grabbed the professor by his collar. He lifted him off the ground, banging his head against the ceiling. He looked him sternly in the eye.

"Do you know who this boy is?" hissed the captain.

"All I know is he's valuable, wanted, and we found him!" shouted the professor as he rubbed his head.

"He's the prince, you fool!" snapped the captain, dropping the professor onto the floor. "We're not handing him over to King Naysayer. We're rescuing him!"

"But that's impossible," said Professor Jones as he snatched the flyer out of Iggy's hand. He looked at the drawing and then back at Iggy. "Do you know the probability of us finding him now, after all this time?"

The captain looked over at Iggy.

"Not in our favor, I reckon, but its true nonetheless."

"It's a miracle," said Miss Blackfeather, smiling.

"It's over a billion to one!" shouted the professor. He grabbed Iggy by the head, turning him this way and that way.

"You're sure he's the prince?" said the professor, not convinced.

"I read his cards," said Miss Blackfeather. "It's him."

"And you expect me to believe he's Prince Rose, just because those dumb cards of yours say so?" scoffed the professor.

Miss Blackfeather rolled her eyes.

"I need hard proof," said the professor, as he continued examining Iggy. He then lifted Iggy's hand. "If he's the prince, where's the ring? King Rose gave him a ring before he handed him over to us."

The captain looked down at Iggy, surprised and confused. "Napoleon said he saw it on him just the other day. That's how he found him."

"CAWWW!" crowed Napoleon.

"The king took the ring from me in class," said Iggy, as he looked at all three of them.

"How convenient," scoffed the professor once again. He took a seat back at his desk. "The kid's not the prince. He's a fraud."

"If this boy says King Naysayer took his ring, then I believe him," growled the captain.

"Well, I can't. I need more than just your beliefs, Captain, and a whole lot more than Miss Blackfeather's magic mumbo jumbo. I'm a scientist. I need evidence."

"Well, how's this for evidence," shouted the captain. "When I was getting beat up by a bunch of knuckleheads, you know who rescued me when he could have just run away? He did!" The captain slapped Iggy on the back. "If that doesn't sound like a princely thing to do, then I don't know what does!"

Miss Blackfeather then stepped up to the

professor's desk. "I know you think everything I believe in is just superstition, but from deep in my heart, to the marrow of my bones, I know this boy is our long-lost prince. And I'm going to do everything in my power to help him regain his throne."

The professor looked at Miss Blackfeather and saw the conviction in her eyes. He then looked past her and at young Iggy. He watched as the young boy lowered his head and shuffled his feet. Could it really be him after all this time? The professor slowly got up from his desk and walked back over to Iggy. He squatted, removed his glasses, and examined the boy once again, turning his head this way and that. He leaned back and stared at Iggy, like he was examining a bug under a microscope. Iggy could tell from the professor's expression that he was thinking very hard. The professor then sighed, put his glasses back on, and stood up.

"You know, statistically, the odds are pretty staggering that he's not the prince." The professor turned to the captain and Miss Blackfeather. He shrugged his shoulders. "But, I guess even science has to follow a hunch once in a while."

The professor then looked down at Iggy and extended his hand. "Nice to see you again, Prince."

Surprised, Iggy looked up at the professor, smiled, and shook his hand.

# Chapter 15

The Broken Heart Tavern was a dimly lit watering hole on the far side of town. Its long oak bar was popular with locals looking to drown their sorrows at the end of a miserable day. When the tavern's bartender saw three strange characters walk into her establishment with a little blonde girl, she shouted: "Hey, this here's a tavern. No children allowed."

"Aye, we'll be out of your hair soon enough," said the captain. He then added, lying: "The girl's come for her father. He's run off again."

As she set a few mugs on the bar, the bartender asked, "What's her daddy's name?"

"Henry O'Henry," replied the captain. "Sensitive fellow with long wavy hair. Prone to reciting verse at the most annoying times."

"Know him well," said the bartender. "He's one of my best customers. He's in the back. He never mentioned he had a daughter."

"Well, he does," Miss Blackfeather sternly replied. "And we've come to make him aware of his responsibilities."

Iggy couldn't believe his luck. Since King Naysayer now offered a huge reward for his capture, Professor Jones came up with the idea of dressing him up as a girl—that way he wouldn't be as easily spotted. Everyone agreed it was a brilliant idea— that is, everyone except Iggy. _He_ didn't like the idea one bit but had a hard time refuting the professor's logical argument. So before they began their search for Henry O'Henry, Miss Blackfeather gave Iggy a pink dress and blonde wig.

"I feel ridiculous," muttered Iggy.

"Well, you look marvelous," whispered Miss Blackfeather as she led him through the tavern. "Who would have thought you'd make such a pretty girl."

Iggy sighed. He never thought discovering he was a prince would mean that he had to dress up like a girl.

As they marched toward the back of the bar, Iggy parted the hair of his blonde wig so he could better see where he was going. He noticed all the people they passed had their heads hung low and were staring deeply into their mugs of ale. Then they came across a group of drunken sailors who had their arms around one another and were singing:

*"Once the seas were calm,*
*Now the seas appear quite rough.*
*Just when I thought I'd seen it all,*
*I realize I ain't seen enough!*
*So hoist the sails, away we go!*
*Another adventure awaits!*
*And before we know it,*
*We'll soon discover,*
*What becomes of our fate!"*

When they reached the back of the tavern, Iggy and the others stopped. They noticed a man snoring loudly, a mug of ale still in his hand. "I got this," said Miss Blackfeather as she walked over to the bar and returned with a bucket of water. She poured it over

Henry O'Henry's head. He jumped up, startled, and wiped his long wet hair from his eyes.

"I don't want any cookies," muttered O'Henry as he stared, blurry eyed, at Iggy.

"What's he talking about?" asked Iggy as he looked up at the others. The captain went to O'Henry and whacked him over the head.

"What'd you do that for?" cried O'Henry.

"To see if I could knock the ale out of you."

As O'Henry rubbed his eyes and looked at each of them, he slowly began to realize whom he was talking to. "What do you all want? I thought we agreed to never see each other again?"

The professor took a seat next to O'Henry and began cleaning his glasses. "That's what we agreed. Yes. But that was because we were working under basic assumptions that have now proven to be false. Therefore, the whole reasoning behind our disbandment must be reevaluated."

Henry O'Henry looked at the captain and then Miss Blackfeather, completely confused. He rubbed his eyes again and asked the little girl standing in front of him, "Do you understand what he's talking about, girl?"

"I ain't no girl," hissed Iggy through clenched teeth.

"I understand. Don't worry. It's okay to be confused," said O'Henry as he lifted the mug of ale to his lips. He was about to take a long gulp when the captain stepped forward and knocked the mug out of his hand, spilling the beer onto the floor.

"What'd you do that for?!" complained Henry O'Henry.

"We ain't got any more time for that," said the captain as he sat down on the other side of the table. Miss Blackfeather motioned to Iggy to take a seat beside her in the remaining chair. O'Henry stared at the group that now surrounded him.

"Like I was trying to explain to you," continued the professor as he put his glasses back on, "new information has come to light which will have a most profound impact on our current situation."

"Why can't you ever talk like a normal person?" asked O'Henry, staring at the professor.

The professor sighed, then leaned back in his chair. "This coming from a poet. I give up."

"Why don't you just leave me alone," O'Henry begged. "I just spent the last money I had on that mug of ale—which you so rudely knocked out of my hand, Captain—_and_ on this." O'Henry reached into a leather satchel hanging from his chair and removed a tiny wooden ship. He placed it on the table in front of them.

The captain quickly snapped up the tiny ship and marveled at it.

Napoleon crowed.

"Aye, Napoleon, she's the spitting image of the

*Lucky Rose,*" said the captain. He peered through the ship's tiny windows and at its little compartments.

Henry O'Henry explained how he thought the ship looked exactly like the *Lucky Rose* as well. When he'd seen it displayed in the window of a pawnshop earlier that day, he'd felt compelled to buy it. Even though he couldn't afford it. The owner of the pawnshop drove a hard bargain, and O'Henry reluctantly agreed to pay the five duckets the man was asking for. Afterward, he came to the tavern and marveled at the little ship's beauty. Then a sadness slowly overwhelmed him. The ship was a reminder of how he'd failed King Rose and the people of the Rose Kingdom.

Miss Blackfeather interrupted O'Henry and whispered, "But that's what we are trying to tell you. We found the prince."

"That's impossible…" began O'Henry.

The professor interrupted. "Improbable, but not impossible."

O'Henry rolled his eyes and asked, "Where?"

"Right here, you darn fool," barked the captain as he pointed a surreptitious finger at Iggy.

O'Henry fixed his eyes on Iggy, noticing his long blonde hair. "I might not be seeing all that clearly, but I thought the prince was a boy. She sure looks an awful lot like a girl."

"I ain't no girl," hissed Iggy again and quickly took off his wig. He stared wide-eyed back at O'Henry, so he could see, without question, he was in fact a boy. Miss Blackfeather quickly grabbed the wig from Iggy and put it back on his head, making sure nobody in the tavern had noticed.

"Now I'm totally confused," said O'Henry with a sigh.

Since Henry O'Henry wasn't catching on, the others explained the situation. They started at the beginning, when Napoleon discovered Iggy at the academy and then alerted the captain. The captain rescued Iggy and took him to Miss Blackfeather and then to Professor Jones. Because everybody in the kingdom was now looking for Iggy, they all agreed—that is, all of them except Iggy—that the best thing to do was dress him up as a girl so nobody in the kingdom would spot him.

After digesting this information, Henry O'Henry responded, "I need another drink." The captain responded with another swift knock to the back of O'Henry's head.

"What's gotten into you, man?" grumbled the captain. "You're Henry O'Henry, the greatest artist this side of the Gargantuan Sea, and here you are wasting your life away in a tavern."

O'Henry stared at the others with a grave expression and sighed. "I _was_ the greatest artist of the Rose Kingdom, the pertinent word being _was_. Since we've come here, I've changed." He looked directly at the professor, the captain, and Miss Blackfeather. "Haven't you all felt different since we've gotten here? Like we are no longer who we once were."

Iggy watched as they all slowly acknowledged that something had indeed changed. The captain then sighed and admitted: "It's true. When those thugs tried to fight me, I couldn't understand why I wasn't able to beat them. I once fought a three-headed dragon off the shores of Lingus with nothing but a teacup, and all of a sudden I wasn't able to battle three buffoons." He then whispered to the others, "If it wasn't for the prince's help, I don't think I would have made it out alive."

Suddenly, O'Henry reached into his leather satchel and unrolled a piece of paper on the table. "I've lost all sense of rhyme and artistic intuition. Without my art, how am I going to inspire people? Yesterday, I tried to draw something and all I could manage was this!"

Iggy and the others stared down at the drawing of a square.

"And you know what the worst part about it is?"

They all shook their heads.

"I was trying to draw a circle."

"That's not the worst part," then chimed in the professor. "I've noticed my power of deduction slipping away from me. The other day I couldn't even add two plus two."

"But that's easy," Iggy replied. "That's four."

"Yes, quite elementary," said the professor sadly, "but it appears my mind is no longer working at maximum capacity. And then I am forced to ask myself the question: without my mind, who am I?"

"Without my art, I'd rather not live…" softly whispered Henry O'Henry.

"Without magic, where's the mystery of it all?" joined in Miss Blackfeather.

"Without my fighting spirit, what kind of captain can I possibly be," lamented Captain Swell. He delicately placed the tiny wooden ship back on the tavern table. "Aye, right now, we are utterly useless."

All four of them sat, quiet and glum. For what felt like an eternity, no one said a word.

"But you're not useless." Iggy finally spoke. "Nobody's useless."

They all looked at the young boy.

"You just need to get your powers back," said Iggy. "Maybe it's the kingdom that is making you all lose your powers? Everybody here is always miserable and thinking and saying negative things. Since you had your powers before you came here, maybe you'll get them back when you leave."

"That does sound logical," said Professor Jones.

"So you just need to find another ship and set sail again," Iggy continued.

Then all of a sudden, Miss Blackfeather smacked the table.

"We don't need to find a ship; we've got one right here." She smiled as she pointed to the small ship resting on the table.

"I guess so," said Iggy, "but don't we need a bigger ship? I mean we're all so big, and it's pretty tiny."

They all sighed again, and the professor nodded in agreement. "The prince does make a solid point. Proportionally, it just won't work."

"I can't take this anymore," said Henry O'Henry as he plopped his head into his hands. "One minute I'm happy; the next minute I'm sad. It's a roller coaster of emotions."

Then Miss Blackfeather slapped the table again. A smirk danced across her lips as she exclaimed, "We've forgotten about the ring!"

# Chapter 16

Miss Blackfeather explained to Iggy and the others how the Royal Rose Ring contained magical powers. If they could get the ring back in Iggy's possession, it should unlock the powers they needed to combat all the negative energy in the kingdom of Naysayer.

"But I had the ring with me my whole time in the academy, and I never noticed any magical powers," said Iggy.

Miss Blackfeather touched Iggy's shoulder. "That's because you didn't believe in yourself. You didn't know how truly special you were," she said. "If you really believed in yourself, the ring would have revealed all its power to you. That's what makes it so special. And that's why the king gave it to you. When the king wore the ring, it granted him the wisdom to be a great leader. It also released a hidden power in all the people the king loved, like his family and royal subjects."

"It's true," said O'Henry. "When I was the king's royal artist, I never felt more inspired. I wanted to paint and write and sculpt every minute of the day."

"Aye," added the captain. "I always felt like wrestling a giant just for the heck of it."

"I must admit," chimed in the professor, "I did come up with more theories while I was in the Rose Kingdom than anywhere else."

Napoleon then crowed loudly, and the captain nodded in agreement. "That's very true, Napoleon. You most certainly were."

"You see," said Miss Blackfeather. "If we can get the prince back his ring, we'll all get our powers back. And when I'm feeling a hundred percent myself, I can easily turn an anthill into a volcano, so turning this tiny ship into a seafaring vessel shouldn't be a problem."

The captain abruptly jumped up from his seat and balanced himself on his wooden leg. Napoleon was so startled that he briefly took to flight, but then landed back on the captain's shoulder. "I like it." The captain beamed. "Now let's get going. Time's wasting."

All of them, except for Iggy, got up from the table.

"What's wrong?" asked Miss Blackfeather.

Iggy looked at them, nervous. "It's just that for all this to work, I have to really believe I'm a prince. I know you all think I am, but I'm not so sure. I just find this all so hard to believe."

They all looked at Iggy. Then Henry O'Henry walked over and gently grabbed Iggy by the shoulders. He stared him straight in the eye. "Each step is a step of faith, Prince. Nobody really knows how the journey is going to end. But I'll tell you what I do know: if you don't believe in yourself, then nobody else will either. You see what I'm getting at, Prince?" said O'Henry.

Iggy thought about what Henry O'Henry had just said. It did make sense. If he didn't believe in himself, why would anybody else?

"Let's give it a shot," Iggy finally said as he looked at the others.

"That's all we can do," O'Henry said with a smile.

# Chapter 17

The ogre responsible for managing the guest list for the king's birthday celebration leafed through his papers one more time. Then he glanced back up at the group standing before him. "You're not on the list," snorted the ogre.

"I've already told you a million times that I know we're not on the list," exclaimed Henry O'Henry. "That's why it's a surprise."

The ogre looked confused and responded, "But I was told not to let anybody in who wasn't on the list."

O'Henry threw back his head in the most dramatic fashion and shouted, "Why me!!!" up to the sky. He then stepped up to the ogre, clutching the tiny wooden ship in one hand and pointing at him with the other. "I'm Henry O'Henry, and my performance troupe is the finest this side of Trafaldor. I've sailed across two seas, and crossed nine continents, because I was commissioned to put on a show for King Naysayer the likes of which he has never seen. If the king finds out that he didn't get to see our show on his birthday, do you know who's going to be in a whole lot of trouble?"

The ogre shook his head no. Henry O'Henry smirked. "Well, the king will blame you. And we all know how the king gets when he's angry."

The ogre glanced one more time at the group before him and noticed the little girl with blonde hair.

"What's the girl do?"

O'Henry glanced down at Iggy, then back at the ogre. "She sings. Finest voice this side of the Ebony Glaciers."

"Let's hear something, then," said the ogre.

"You mean right now?" asked O'Henry.

"Yep," said the ogre.

O'Henry shook his head. "Nope. Only during performance. I don't want her straining her vocal cords."

"If she don't sing…" The ogre smirked. "Then you don't get inside."

All eyes stared down at Iggy. Iggy gulped. He had never sung a song in his life. "Well, go ahead, little girl," prodded the ogre. "Sing something, if you're as good as he says you are."

Iggy didn't know what to do. He looked at O'Henry and noticed a bead of sweat running down his face. O'Henry then nodded, motioning to Iggy to do as the ogre asked.

Iggy closed his eyes. "Here goes anything," he thought to himself. He began to sing a song he'd heard some of the kids sing at the academy. As he sang, his voice cracked several times. Iggy couldn't see that everyone in hearing distance had covered his or her ears. After finishing his song, he opened his eyes and looked around. He was surprised to see that the guard had plugged his ears with his fat ogre fingers and had squeezed his eyes shut. Henry O'Henry and the others had done the same.

The guard then slowly opened his eyes and unplugged his ears and begged, "Are you finally finished, girlie?"

Iggy, who couldn't wait to take off his outfit and stop being called a girl, nodded that he was done.

"Thank heavens!" said the guard as he turned to O'Henry. "She's terrible. I can't let her sing for the king. The king might go deaf. Sorry, I can't let you in. Best get a move on now." The guard motioned to the other guards under his command. They escorted Iggy and his friends away.

# Chapter 18

While Iggy was busy singing for the guard, he didn't know that an army of rats was scurrying around the kingdom of Naysayer looking for him. The rats, led by Teddy, snuck into every crack of every building and looked in every dark corner of every room. But they could not find Iggy anywhere.

"Why is it so difficult to find such a stupid, smelly, ugly kid like Iggy?" angrily thought Teddy. He started worrying that he might never find Iggy and that Miss Spitfire would punish him by keeping him in rat form forever.

Teddy wasn't the only one who was worried that Iggy hadn't been found yet. Perhaps even more worried than Teddy was Miss Spitfire, who that evening was in the royal banquet hall celebrating the king's 45th, hmmm, I mean 25th birthday.

Miss Spitfire watched as the king shook hands with the arriving guests. Normally, the king would be in a good mood on his birthday. After all, there was only one thing that the king liked more than money, and that was presents. And on his birthday, he usually received more presents than you and I could possibly imagine. But Miss Spitfire noticed that _this_ year, the king didn't really care about the gifts he received. When Prince JoyStick gave the king the newest, most amazing video game as a gift, King Naysayer quickly tossed the game into a corner of the room. So far, it was quite apparent that the king was not enjoying his birthday at all. And Miss Spitfire knew why, which made her very nervous.

"All these presents suck," complained the king to Miss Spitfire. "I want that little brat Iggy and all the money he's worth. That's what I want for my birthday. Have you found him yet?"

"Not yet, Your Highness, but it should be any moment now," said Miss Spitfire, praying she was right.

"I've offered one million duckets for his capture," said the king. "And not a single Naysayer has found him." Then he stared at Miss Spitfire. "You better hope we find him soon, Spitfire, or my birthday will be a disaster, and the only enjoyment I will get will be in implementing some of my new torture techniques on you."

Miss Spitfire's bony knees began to shake. She promised the king that Iggy would be found.

"Well, I'm starting to lose patience," said

the king. He walked away from Miss Spitfire as more guests began to arrive. As she watched King Naysayer greet the king and queen of the kingdom of Fashion, Miss Spitfire wondered how such a miserable little boy like Iggy could possibly be a prince. Then she realized there _were_ certain things that made him different from the rest of the children she taught at the academy. For example, all the other children did what she instructed without question; Iggy did not. He wanted to know the _why_ behind everything. And since Miss Spitfire really didn't like to explain herself, she turned to beating Iggy with her walking staff instead. That usually did the trick, and he eventually stopped asking so many questions. "He was a strange kid," Miss Spitfire thought to herself, "but a prince, I still don't believe it."

# Chapter 19

Iggy felt bad about letting the others down. "Sorry I have such a terrible voice," he said as they walked away from the guard.

"Aye, don't worry about it, Prince," said the captain. He slapped Iggy on the back. Iggy stumbled slightly, forcing him to adjust his wig. "If they had asked me to sing, I probably would have cracked a few windows. I have a surprisingly high-pitched voice for such a burly man of action."

Napoleon crowed.

"Quiet, you," muttered the captain.

After a long trek, Iggy and his friends finally arrived on the other side of Naysayer Castle. Iggy parted his long blonde wig and looked up. The castle stretched high into the sky. It was painted black and gray, like the dark cloud that hung over the Naysayer Academy. Pointy spires shot up from the castle and needled the stars in the night sky. Iggy then noticed, atop the castle's high walls, the statues of lions, alligators, and bears glaring down at him. Their mouths were wide open, as if they were ready to take a bite. The sight of the mean-looking animal statues sent a shiver through his body. "They look alive," Iggy thought to himself.

From inside the castle, Iggy and the others heard music and laughter.

"It looks like most of the guards are inside celebrating," whispered Henry O'Henry.

"That's good for us," said Professor Jones.

Napoleon crowed once again.

"Be quiet, Napoleon!" muttered the captain. "We don't want any attention."

Professor Jones looked up at the animal statues on the high castle walls and had an idea. He wasn't sure if it was a good idea, because he now doubted his intellect so much, but he thought it best to mention it anyway. Professor Jones had brought a long rope with him. He asked the captain if he'd be able to lasso the rope over one of the statues that hovered high above.

"That's like asking a baker if he can bake cookies," said the captain.

The professor looked confused. "I don't know; can he?"

"Give me that rope," grunted the captain.

They stood back as the captain twirled the rope high above his head and then let it loose. The rope shot up into the night sky. They held their breath as they watched the lasso sail toward the statue of a bear and then sling itself over the bear's head. Once he made sure the rope was secure, the captain told the others to start climbing.

# Chapter 20

**O**nce over the castle wall, Iggy and his friends snuck around until they found a window that looked down into the king's banquet hall. What they saw amazed them. Down below was the most incredible party any of them had ever seen. King Naysayer, never known to be stingy when it came to his birthday, had thrown a birthday celebration to rival all others. There were jugglers juggling, ballerinas dancing, and magicians performing magic. There were even monkeys performing tricks. And at one end of the hall, Iggy spotted the white elephant he had seen earlier on the dock. The elephant just stood there quietly, very sadly watching the party before him.

Then Iggy noticed the food. There was food everywhere! Big plates of it, and all the king's guests were devouring it by the mouthfuls. Iggy's stomach growled.

Henry O'Henry, who still held the small wooden ship in his hand, pointed toward the far end of the banquet hall. "Look! There's the king."

Iggy saw King Naysayer sitting at the head of a very long table. The king looked very bored. He yawned as he picked at his food and then took a sip of wine from a golden goblet.

"Look. There's the ring," said the captain. He pointed to the king's hand, which was now clutching a large turkey leg.

Iggy looked closely. He saw the bright red ring wrapped around the king's pudgy, short finger. "That's going to be tough to get off of him," Iggy said out loud. He then turned to the others. "Is that really the only way you will get your powers back?" he asked. "I really don't see how we're going to get that off of him, and not get caught."

Miss Blackfeather cleared her throat. "Well, you see, Prince, _we_ can't actually do anything. It's up to you now."

"What are you talking about?" asked Iggy suspiciously.

"Well, the way it works, you see, is that the only person who can touch the Rose Ring is you. If we touch it, it loses all its power," explained Miss Blackfeather.

"What?!" Iggy said in shock. "And you decided to tell me this now!"

"It's the legend of the ring," said Miss Blackfeather apologetically. "Now...legends can be proven false, but I usually don't like to mess with them. You see, according to legend, if anyone other than the true heir to the Rose Ring touches it, the ring will lose all its power."

"But if the king's already touched it, hasn't it already lost all its power?" asked Iggy.

Miss Blackfeather shook her head. "The king isn't one of your royal subjects. We are. If any person from the Rose Kingdom, other than its rightful heir, touches it, then the ring becomes merely a plain old ring."

"Now, that's what I call a dramatic revelation, don't you think?" added O'Henry.

"And...following that strain of logic..." slowly deducted the professor, "it means the only person who can get the ring off King Naysayer is the prince."

"That's what we've been saying all along!" said O'Henry as he slapped Professor Jones over the head for stating the obvious.

"I'm sorry," apologized the professor as he wiped his glasses. "I feel my intellect growing weaker and weaker with every passing minute."

Iggy turned and looked back at King Naysayer and the Rose Ring that was squeezed tightly onto his finger. He then noticed Miss Spitfire, looking around the hall, tapping her walking staff on the ground. Iggy had hoped he would never see her again.

"There's one more teeny little thing," said Miss Blackfeather.

"What now?" asked Iggy. He turned and looked at Miss Blackfeather, slightly annoyed that he was being told all this information at the very last minute.

"Like I said earlier," said Miss Blackfeather, "the ring will only unleash its power if you really believe you are our prince."

Napoleon crowed.

"Napoleon's right," said the captain. "You got to believe you're a prince, or none of this will work."

Iggy noticed they were all staring at him with hopeful expressions. He remained quiet for a moment. He really wanted to believe he was a prince, but deep down, he still wasn't sure. He then thought about what O'Henry had said in the tavern: how you have to believe in yourself before anybody else will. Iggy inhaled deeply and finally said, "Well, I guess I'd rather believe I'm a prince than believe I'm Stinky Iggy."

"That's good enough for me!" exclaimed O'Henry. "Now go down there and get back that ring!"

Iggy turned and looked down at the crowded banquet hall, then at King Naysayer and Miss Spitfire one more time. "But the minute I try to get the ring off the king's finger, I'll be found out. I won't be able to get out of there."

Miss Blackfeather touched Iggy's shoulder and said, "The second you get the ring off King Naysayer, slip it on your finger right away. Once the ring is on your finger, and you truly believe you're our prince, we'll all get our powers back. Then I can use my magic to make you invisible, so you can sneak out of the banquet hall without anybody seeing you."

"Are you sure this is going to work?" asked Iggy.

"No," said Miss Blackfeather. She looked Iggy squarely in the eye. "That's why it's an adventure."

# Chapter 21

Luckily for Iggy, there was only one guard watching the main entrance into the banquet hall. And when the guard wasn't looking, Iggy snuck past him. Captain Swell and the others watched him, hidden behind a stone pillar in the distance. The moment he snuck inside the large hall, Iggy quickly dropped to his knees and scurried underneath a nearby table. He made sure he didn't touch anybody's feet, so they wouldn't notice him.

He began crawling from underneath the first table to another, sneaking his way toward the king. When he was near the king's table, he lifted the tablecloth and saw Miss Spitfire sitting nearby. He was both scared and angry at the sight of the mean old woman. Iggy wondered, "How am I going to sneak from this table to the king's table without having her see me?"

Then suddenly, Iggy heard the king shout as he got up from his chair: "It's my birthday and I'm bored. I want to see that elephant do some tricks!"

One of the king's guards hurried over to the far end of the room and struck the large white elephant with a whip. The elephant, hurting from the blow, blew a huge gust of air from its trunk. The last thing this elephant wanted to do was perform, and Iggy felt sorry for it as he watched the elephant drag its huge body onto one leg and balance a red ball on its trunk. Everyone in the banquet hall stood up and turned to watch the elephant—including the king and Miss Spitfire. And with Miss Spitfire's back turned away, Iggy saw his chance to sneak underneath the king's table undetected. While the guests cheered for the elephant, Iggy quickly crawled out from underneath his table, scurried behind Miss Spitfire's chair, and slid underneath the king's table.

After breathing a sigh of relief, Iggy saw the king sit back in his chair. He looked at the king's big round belly. He then turned and saw that Miss Spitfire had taken her seat as well. He noticed her bony knees and pointy black boots. Being so close to the king and Miss Spitfire made him very nervous. He needed to get the Rose Ring off of the king's finger quickly and leave the banquet hall at once. But how was he going to slip the ring off the king's finger without getting noticed?

Iggy had an idea. A white napkin rested on the king's lap. He crawled up to the king's chair, snatched the napkin, and tossed it onto the floor. After a few minutes, the king noticed that his napkin had fallen off his lap and reached down with his hand to pick it up. That's when Iggy saw his chance.

As the king's pudgy hand reached down to fetch the napkin, the Rose Ring sparkled into view. Iggy quickly grabbed onto the king's hand and tried to slide the ring off his finger. But the ring wouldn't budge! It was squeezed on too tight! Then suddenly, Iggy felt himself getting dragged from underneath the table.

"Well, what do we have here?" said the king. He lifted Iggy up by his dress. "It looks like I've caught myself a little girl who also happens to be a thief." Everyone in the banquet hall gasped. The musicians stopped playing, the jugglers stopped juggling, and the elephant stopped balancing his red ball.

"I'm not a girl!" screamed Iggy as he threw off his wig. "I'm Prince Iggy, and the Rose Ring belongs to me!"

"I knew it!" said Miss Spitfire when she saw Iggy. She quickly hurried to the king's side. "See, Your Highness, I told you I'd find him." She then turned her evil eyes toward Iggy. "I'm going to give you the biggest beating you've ever had in your life!"

"The Rose Ring belongs to me!" shouted Iggy to the king.

The king looked around as the banquet hall grew silent. He cleared his throat. "Seems like we have a very confused little boy here," said the king to everyone in the hall.

"It's the truth," shouted Iggy. "I'm Prince Rose, and you stole my ring."

King Naysayer noticed his guests whispering to one another. The king had hoped to keep the truth about Iggy a secret, until he had contacted Queen Victoria personally. But now, with Iggy's very public proclamation, the king realized that one of the guests might send word to Queen Victoria without his knowledge. He needed to act quickly and discredit the young boy before word spread that Iggy might be the long-lost Prince Rose.

"Did you hear that, Miss Spitfire? This thief thinks this ring belongs to him. Isn't that the most ridiculous thing you've ever heard?"

"Yes, it is," said Miss Spitfire as she poked Iggy with her staff. "He's nothing but a useless little liar!"

"I'm not useless!" shouted Iggy at the top of his lungs. "I'm Prince Rose of the Rose Kingdom."

"Ha, Prince Rose of the Rose Kingdom?!" nervously giggled the king. "Now, that's possibly the most ridiculous thing I've ever heard. You're no prince! There's absolutely nothing special about you at all. Why, even a cockroach is more special than you." The king continued chuckling and grew relieved when some guests in the banquet hall began joining him. "My young, worthless little boy," continued the king, hoping to discredit Iggy once and for all. "This ring belongs to me, and when you steal something from the king, do you know what happens?"

"No," said Iggy as he looked down at the floor. He knew he wasn't going to like what he was about to hear.

"Can anyone help him?" asked the king, addressing his guests.

A man stood up in the back of the hall and shouted, "You make him eat mud for a whole month, and then make him stand on his hands until he throws up!"

"No, that's not it," said the king.

Then a woman stood up from her table. "You make him wear nothing but purple for a whole year."

"Nope, but that's an interesting idea. No, my dear guests," said the king, holding Iggy up for all to see. "When somebody tries to steal from me, he gets sent to the Black Tower...where the Wheel of Tears awaits."

"The Wheel of Tears! I knew that!" said a man as he angrily threw his napkin onto his table.

Iggy couldn't speak. He had never heard of the Wheel of Tears, but he didn't like the sound of it.

"You see, ladies and gentleman," continued the king, still holding Iggy, "this is why I believe in strict punishment for our Naysayer youth. We can't be soft when it comes to children. Only by showing them a hard hand can we hope to live in a civil society."

All the guests nodded their heads in agreement. They looked at Iggy with disappointment. Iggy then saw Miss Spitfire staring straight at him. She leaned over and whispered in his ear. "And when the king and his Wheel of Tears gets done with you, you're going right back to the academy. I'm going to make your life more miserable than you can ever imagine."

Iggy lowered his head and let out a big sigh. Was this how his adventure was going to end? Was he going back to the miserable place where it started? Then Iggy had a very sad thought: Perhaps he would always be a miserable boy after all. Maybe all this talk about the Rose Ring and him being a prince was one big joke. Iggy felt like crying.

Then suddenly someone screamed.

"It's a rat!"

# Chapter 22

Iggy looked up. An army of rats streamed through the banquet hall entrance. All the guests screamed and jumped up on top of their tables. The white elephant—which was deathly afraid of mice—began stomping around the hall. Iggy realized this distraction could provide him his last chance to see if he was truly a prince. While everyone in the banquet hall was screaming and shouting, Iggy firmly planted his foot on the king's face and tried to yank the Rose Ring off the king's fat finger.

"Stop that! Stop that!" shouted the king.

Iggy pulled harder and harder. And with one final pull, the ring slid off the king's finger and flew into the air. The king quickly dropped Iggy. They both watched as the ring sailed across the banquet hall, and then dropped to the floor and rolled away. Iggy ran after the ring.

"Get that ring!" shouted the king to his guards. "And get that boy too!"

As Iggy chased after the ring, he heard Miss Spitfire yell: "Teddy! Get that ring!"

Teddy, who was leading the charge of rats heading toward Iggy, quickly changed direction. He followed the ring as it rolled across the banquet floor. He was about to snatch it with his sharp rat teeth, when suddenly the terrified white elephant—which had been frantically storming through the hall—blocked his way with its big white hoof.

Iggy watched as the ring hit a crack in the floor and bounced back into the air. He jumped onto a table and leaped after it. In flight, Iggy stretched his arms and caught the ring. When he landed on the ground, he quickly slid the ring onto his finger. He closed his eyes tightly and said: "I'm Prince Rose, and my loyal subjects are Captain Bartholomew Swell, Miss Blackfeather, Professor Jones, and Henry O'Henry. As their prince, I command they get their powers back!" Iggy believed what he said so deeply that beads of sweat formed on his face. His heart pounded in his chest. He wasn't a miserable little boy. He was a prince! He knew the truth. That was all that mattered.

Suddenly, Iggy felt something very strange begin to happen. His body was tingling. Then he began shrinking. "I thought Miss Blackfeather said she was going to make me invisible," Iggy nervously thought to himself. "I'm shrinking! I'm not invisible! Miss Blackfeather must have used a shrinking spell instead of an invisible spell by accident." Iggy kept shrinking and shrinking, until he was the same size as the tiniest rat in the banquet hall. And now that he was so small, a rat could easily eat him for dinner with one quick bite! So when Iggy saw a group of rats heading straight for him, he started running as quickly as he could.

Then Iggy heard Captain Swell shout: "Prince, run toward the ship!"

Iggy turned and saw the captain at the other end of the room. He was tiny like him too! The tiny captain pointed to the tiny wooden ship, which lay on the floor of the banquet hall in the distance. Iggy was now _so_ small that the ship seemed very far away, but he ran toward it as fast as he could. He could hear the ear-piercing squeaks of the rats close behind him.

Then he heard Miss Spitfire shout: "Children, stop him!"

Up ahead, Iggy saw Teddy charging straight at him. He could tell it was Teddy by the look in the rat's eyes. It was the same look he used to see right before getting beaten up at the academy. Teddy opened his mouth wide, so his rat teeth could take a good bite out of Iggy. Iggy closed his eyes, ready to be eaten.

Then suddenly, he heard the captain bark: "Not so fast, you nasty rodent!"

Iggy opened his eyes and saw the captain running toward him, waving a huge turkey leg over his head. The captain jumped in the air and smashed the turkey leg over Teddy's head!

"Ow," squeaked Teddy, stopping in his tracks.

The captain grabbed Iggy by the hand, and the two of them ran toward the ship. Professor Jones, Henry O'Henry, and Miss Blackfeather were already waiting for them. Once Iggy and the captain finally made it on board, Miss Blackfeather turned to them and apologized. "Sorry about the shrinking spell," she said. "I got nervous in all the excitement, but this one should get us out of here. I promise." Miss Blackfeather then closed her eyes and began to recite another spell:

*"Oh, ship, oh, ship*
*Fly high into the air*
*We found our prince*
*Now get us out of here!"*

Suddenly, the tiny wooden ship began to float. Higher and higher it went, until it nearly touched the ceiling of the king's banquet hall. Everyone in the room, including Miss Spitfire and the king, looked up in amazement.

The captain ran to the front of the ship and took the ship's steering wheel into his hands. "Now let's get out of here!" he yelled. The captain steered the floating ship toward one of the windows of the banquet hall. The ship crashed through the window and floated into the night sky. Everyone inside the castle stormed outside and watched this most incredible sight. The tiny ship floated over the heads of all the Naysayers in the kingdom, eventually making its way past the Naysayer Docks and over the sea. When the ship was finally a safe distance from the shore, it plopped down into the water.

Iggy turned and looked at Miss Blackfeather, who was standing at the far corner of the ship's deck with her eyes closed, concentrating.

> *"Oh, powers, oh, powers*
> *Mysterious you be.*
> *Once we were small,*
> *Now make us big like a tree!"*

Then an even more incredible thing happened. The ship began to grow. It kept getting bigger and bigger. Then, not only did the ship start to get bigger, but Iggy and all his friends started to grow too. They kept growing and growing until they were back to their normal size.

Iggy and his friends looked back at the kingdom of Naysayer. A huge crowd had gathered on the docks and was shouting at them. Iggy saw the king and Miss Spitfire among them.

On the dock, King Naysayer angrily turned to

Miss Spitfire and screamed, "Can't you do anything with that staff of yours! They're getting away!"

Miss Spitfire looked at her walking staff and sighed. "Like I told you before, Your Royal Highness, I'm afraid not. It can only turn people into rats. Now that Iggy really believes he's a prince, he's much too powerful for this little thing."

Miss Spitfire took her walking staff in her hands and snapped it in half. Teddy, who was still a rat and resting near Miss Spitfire's feet, squeaked in horror. "Oh, I'm sorry, Teddy," said Miss Spitfire, realizing what she had done. "I guess you'll have to stay a rat forever."

# Chapter 23

**B**ack on the ship, the captain smiled at Iggy as he turned the ship's wheel. He was happy to have a seafaring vessel under his command again. "Ready to make your way back home, Prince?" he asked. The captain pointed to a red star in the distance. "If we follow the Rose Star, we should be home before you know it. Maybe on the way, we can take a dip in the Blue Diamond Falls," he added.

Iggy walked up beside the captain. He looked up at the night sky and the millions of stars shining brightly. He noticed the Rose Star burning bright red among them all. Miss Blackfeather, Professor Jones, and Henry O'Henry then joined them at the front of the ship. Iggy looked away from the star and back at his friends. "I can't believe it's true. I'm really a prince after all."

The captain placed his hand on Iggy's shoulder. "That's right. You're a prince through and through."

"CAWWW," crowed Napoleon.

"That's right, Napoleon," said the captain. "You just needed to believe in yourself."

Iggy smiled, big and wide. He looked at his friends and then at the ocean in front of him. There were so many different places to go and adventures to have. And now that he believed he was a prince, Iggy realized there was nothing stopping him.

# What's Next for Prince Iggy

Iggy and his friends set sail for the Rose Kingdom. But Iggy isn't sure if he has what it takes to really be a prince. Well, he's about to find out…

When the *Lucky Rose 2* blasts off into space, Iggy meets the Rose Star and literally has an out-of-body experience. And that's just the beginning. His adventures include confronting a hungry shark face-to-face, dancing in a live-or-die talent competition, and battling a blue dragon with very clean teeth.

And when Iggy finally makes it to the Rose Kingdom, Queen Victoria refuses to give up the throne. If Iggy wants to become ruler of the Rose Kingdom, he must enter the Tower of Decisions. Only problem is, very few people make it out alive…

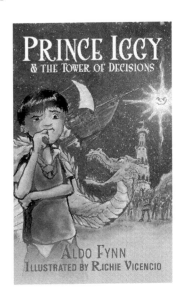

"This delightful, adventurous story shows even royal princes feel self-doubt sometimes...Fynn uses this volume to address adolescent anxiety and self-doubt... Fynn is more than adept at lightening the mood with a heavy dose of absurdity...As the novel ends with a cliffhanger, readers of all ages will be anxious to see what adventures are next for the Rose prince."
– *Foreword Clarion Reviews*

"Offers excitement and surprises to keep young readers engaged. The evocative dreamy, tonal illustrations of varying sizes that are scattered throughout the book are visually enticing and complement the narrative by effectively capturing the emotions of the characters. *Prince Iggy and the Tower of Decisions* offers a magical adventure and some wonderful lessons for young children." – *IndieReader*

## Picture Books by Aldo Fynn

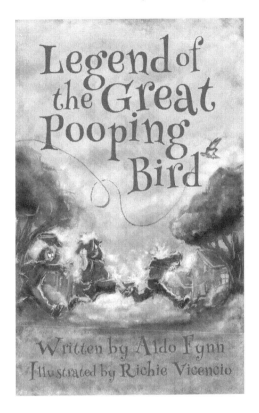

In this funny, rhyming picture book, children learn a sticky yet valuable lesson about bullying. Children and parents will delight in reading this wacky tale out loud.

## Picture Books by Aldo Fynn

Waldo learns a valuable lesson about controlling his temper when a fly interrupts his violin playing. Children and parents will fall in love with this rhyming picture book.

## About the Author

ALDO FYNN enjoys writing wacky, fantastical stories. He lives under his desk. You can contact him at aldofynn@gmail.com.

He hopes you enjoyed reading this book. *Prince Iggy and the Kingdom of Naysayer* is the first book in The Adventures of Prince Iggy series. It's followed by *Prince Iggy and the Tower of Decisions.*

If you enjoyed reading about Prince Iggy, please leave an honest review on Amazon. Aldo appreciates your feedback.

## About the Illustrator

RICHIE VICENCIO lives in Jersey City, New Jersey. He has worked as an illustrator and storyboard artist for various ad agencies, filmmakers, and video-game publishers. His portfolio is available at www.littlerisingson.com.